THE SPIRIT FLYER SERIES

THE TOY CAMPAIGN

The Plot to Trick a Town with Toys

JOHN BIBEE

Illustrated by Paul Turnbaugh

INTERVARSITY PRESS
DOWNERS GROVE, ILLINOIS 60515

InterVarsity Press is the book-publishing division of InterVarsity Christian Fellowship, a student movement active on campus at hundreds of universities, colleges and schools of nursing. For information about local and regional activities, write Public Relations Dept., InterVarsity Christian Fellowship, 6400 Schroeder Rd., P.O. Box 7895, Madison, WI 53707-7895.

Cover illustration: Paul Turnbaugh

ISBN 0-8308-1201-6

Printed in the United States of America

Library of Congress Cataloging in Publication Data

Bibee, John.

    The toy campaign.

    (The Spirit Flyer series ; 2)

    Summary: Armed with only her magic Spirit Flyer bicycle, Susan takes on the owner of a toy shop who is offering free toys to children in order to lure them into the Deeper World.

    [1. Fantasy] I. Title. II. Series: Bibee, John. Spirit Flyer series ; 2.

PZ7.B471464To   1987   [Fic]   87-3261

ISBN 0-8308-1201-6

17	16	15	14	13	12	11	10	9	8	7	6	5
99	98	97	96	95	94	93						

*This book is for Doug Heimburger
and a number of friends
who gave me time to write
through their generous support.
My thanks to you all.*

WHEN THE
TOY STORE
CLOSED

· · · · · · · ·

1

Some children wish for toys all their lives, thinking that toys hold a secret magic treasure. The search for the perfect toy may take them into many worlds. But when their journey enters the Deeper World, they may be surprised at what they find.

One summer there was a town full of children who wished for toys and toys and more toys. And one day, their wishes seemed to be coming true . . .

Something unusual was going on in the toy store that summer, but no one knew what it was until it was almost too late.

10

The toy store in Centerville had closed suddenly. Almost every child around was puzzled because it was the third week of summer vacation, and somehow it just didn't seem right that the only toy store in town was closed for so long. A sign in the window spelled out the bad news:

****

CLOSED UNTIL FURTHER NOTICE

****

Big black curtains had been placed across the front windows inside the entire store. Parents had been calling Mr. Potter, the owner of the toy store, but Mr. Potter was never at home. His house seemed as empty as the toy store.

Each day several children in town would walk or ride their bicycles to the store. The children would press their faces against the big glass windows hoping to see some sign of activity beyond the heavy black curtains. But for two weeks they saw nothing.

Susan Kramar was curious about the closing of the toy store, but not as curious as her cousin John. John Kramar made a daily trip to the store because he had a secret reason for wanting to know what was going on. No one thought it unusual that he would stop by there each day since so many other children did the same thing.

But Susan noticed John's frequent trips. She had been worried about her cousin for several days. For three weeks he had been acting odd, though the changes in his behavior were hard to explain. He would go through moods, up and down, like a bouncing basketball. One minute he would be happy and goofing off. The next minute he would fall into a quiet mood, seeming depressed and worried.

When John was feeling good, his self-confidence was often annoying to Susan because he acted like a know-it-all. And when he was down, he was sometimes irritable. The two cousins had lived together ever since John was small when his parents disappeared in a storm. But now Susan didn't think she knew him anymore. Nor could she figure out why he was so interested in the toy store.

Susan and John usually got along pretty well, even though only a year separated them. They had formed a lawn-mowing business together that summer and had started to make good money. But John's brooding about the toy store and sudden mood changes got on Susan's nerves. She was a careful worker and did most of the trimming and clipping when they worked on a lawn. She thought John was careless in general, but for the past week he had been more careless than ever. When he was happy, he rushed too much and did a poor job cutting the grass. When he was in a bad mood, he took forever to finish even the simplest task. Susan felt as if she were doing her job and half of John's job too.

On a Monday morning, the last day of June, she planned to tell John to shape up, or she was going to get another partner. She figured she would give him until Friday, July the Fourth, to change or else. But before she got a chance to tell him, John told her his plan to unlock the toy store mystery, and that's how the whole adventure started.

"All I want to do is look in that little window that's in the alley behind the store," John told Susan. He seemed eager and confident. But at the same time Susan felt as if he were holding back or hiding something.

Susan was in the garage putting oil on the chain of her new bicycle which was really an old red bicycle. Five other old red bicycles were parked in the garage. Though each one was slightly different in size and shape, they all had the same name painted in noble white letters on the side: "Spirit Flyer."

"But why do you need me to go to the toy store?" Susan asked.

"I just want someone to be there," John said. "Someone with a Spirit Flyer. That's why I'm not asking Roger."

Since John didn't want to ask Roger, his best friend, Susan knew John must be serious about wanting her to go along. Though she was glad

that he trusted her, she knew John had a bad habit of jumping into things carelessly. Her mother called John impulsive.

"It sounds rather impulsive to me," Susan said, trying to sound like her mother. "And it seems awful snoopy, like it's not quite legal."

"Why do you have to be so serious and sensible all the time?" John complained.

"I just don't want to do something dumb or wrong," Susan said defensively. "Besides, what does the toy store have to do with our Spirit Flyers?"

"I'm not sure yet," John said. "I just thought you'd understand more, because you know about Spirit Flyers and about the Deeper World. And about the time I disappeared."

Susan looked up. Almost three weeks earlier, the day before the toy store had closed, John Kramar had impatiently hooked up a gear lever to his Spirit Flyer bicycle without getting help. Now John knew Spirit Flyer bicycles were Magic, but even he wasn't prepared for what happened when he pressed the gear lever that was hooked up the wrong way. He disappeared right before his family's eyes into thin air and he didn't return until three hours later. And when he came back, his T-shirt and jeans were torn and dirty and covered with a dirty black powder than looked and smelled like soot or ashes.

John had not said much about his mysterious adventure. He claimed he couldn't remember where he went or what had happened. But Susan wondered if that was true. She thought something had happened on the strange trip which had made the eleven-year-old boy afraid.

When John returned from that secret journey, he immediately took the gear lever off his bike. The boy refused to touch it or the horn, the mirror or the other old bicycle accessories he had removed when he had first found it at the dump.

"What does the toy store have to do with the Deeper World and you disappearing?" Susan asked.

"Probably nothing," John replied. "But then again . . ."

14

Susan stared at John. He seemed fidgety and nervous. She was certain he was holding back something.

"Why don't you tell us what happened when you disappeared?" Susan asked in a soft voice. "And why don't you let me help you hook up the instruments to your Spirit Flyer? Grandfather Kramar told us your accessories hook up exactly the same way they are attached to our Spirit Flyers."

"I wish Grandfather didn't have to go on that trip to see Aunt Thelma," John said. "People get sick at the worst times. It's unfair."

"Great Aunt Thelma couldn't help it," Susan said. "Besides, Grandfather told us it would be all right and that you should put the instruments back on because a Spirit Flyer isn't really complete without them. He said it was very important."

"I don't care if it's complete or important," John said irritably. His happy mood suddenly snapped and the boy looked worried.

Susan sighed. She had tried several different times to convince John that he should put the gear lever and the other instruments back on. The boy hardly seemed to trust the old red bicycle anymore, Susan thought to herself.

"We don't really know what all those instruments do," John complained. "Besides, it works well enough for me without the instruments. I've done ok, haven't I? I mean, after all, I saved the day when I caught those two thieves who stole all the bicycles in town, didn't I? I made the front page of the *Centerville Times* that week, if you remember."

"You've only reminded us a thousand times over the last three weeks," Susan groaned. John was suddenly confident again, and irritating in a different way. The town had treated him like a hero, but the praise had only gone to the boy's head. John acted like he had practically saved the whole town and half the county too. Susan thought any kind of bragging was annoying, but this was especially irritating since it was John's magic bicycle, the Spirit Flyer, which was really responsible for catching the thieves. John was merely along for the ride, Susan thought. She had to admit she was somewhat jealous of all the attention John had received. But even so, John's bragging was still inexcusable.

"I'm not saying your Spirit Flyer isn't wonderful the way it is right now," Susan said slowly. "But it seems like you're limiting the bike when you don't put on the accessories."

"I know, I know," John said impatiently. "Why do you keep bugging me? I had all I needed when I caught those bicycle thieves, didn't I?"

"Well, I'm not going to argue with you about it," Susan said as she put the oil can and rags away. She shrugged her shoulders. "Grandfather said everyone learns at their own pace. And you've been warned. You could at least read some in *The Book of the Kings* Grandfather gave us. There's all sorts of neat stories and things in there about the Deeper World and the Three Kings and Spirit Flyers."

"Have you read the whole book?" John demanded.

"Not yet," Susan admitted. "But I'm reading a little at a time and it's really neat. Some parts are hard to understand, but a lot of the book is just as—"

"I just don't feel like reading it, that's all," John interrupted. The mere size of the book discouraged John. And in those days, right after being a hero for catching the bicycle thieves, he thought he already knew more than enough about the Spirit Flyer and the things of the Deeper World.

"Will you help me look in the toy store window or not?" John asked impatiently.

"I'll go along, but I don't know how much I'll help," Susan said. "If you think that the toy store has something to do with the Deeper World or Spirit Flyers, maybe you should tell Dad."

"There's nothing to tell, yet," John said. "Besides, if there really is something deeper going on, he probably wouldn't want me to investigate at all. You know how he is. He seems almost afraid to ride his Spirit Flyer."

"Well, they aren't ordinary bicycles," Susan said and smiled.

She had been supremely happy ever since the day the Spirit Flyers had come to her family. During the three hours John had disappeared, the old red bicycles simply appeared in the Kramar's garage, like gifts waiting under a Christmas tree. The bikes were indeed very special gifts from the Three Kings. Yet Spirit Flyers were more than just bicycles; they were a sign that each owner belonged to the Kingdom of the Kings.

Susan didn't know how she had ever lived without her Spirit Flyer. Even though she had ridden it for just a few weeks, the old red bicycle seemed like a close friend. Each ride made her feel she was about to start a new adventure. Perhaps it was because the bikes were so mysterious and so powerful that Susan's parents had both been hesitant to ride them as often as their children.

Mr. Kramar was especially cautious about riding his old red bicycle. Because of John's disappearance, Mr. Kramar didn't want anyone to use the gear levers on the Spirit Flyers until they understood more about them. He had read some in *The Book of the Kings* about Spirit Flyers, but as sheriff for the town of Centerville, he often felt too busy or too tired to read about the ways and gifts of the kings. Susan and her sisters had sadly agreed not to use the gear levers for the time being. And John didn't have to agree since he had taken the gear lever off his bike.

"Even if Spirit Flyers aren't ordinary bicycles, I don't think we should be afraid of them, the way Dad seems to be," Susan said. "I guess he thinks something might happen that we can't control."

"Well, you never know what will happen for sure when you ride a Spirit Flyer," John said, speaking from experience. "You *can't* control them like a regular bike."

"But as long as you hold on, they're safe," Susan said. "That's what Grandfather Kramar told us. Even though you disappeared, you got back ok."

"Sure," John said, though not too confidently. "But I don't want to talk about that again. Let's go down to the toy store before it gets too hot."

"Ok," Susan said and sighed. She felt like she was going against her better judgment, but deep inside, John's talk and behavior made her wonder if something unusual was happening at the toy store. She decided she would wait to speak to him about doing his share of the work in the lawn-mowing business. She hoped that if he felt more settled about the toy store, then maybe he would get his mind back on his work.

As Susan lifted up the garage door, the uneasy feeling inside made her pause.

"Maybe I am too serious about things," Susan argued with herself. "But then why do I feel as if we're about to get into some kind of trouble?"

She pushed her heavy old Spirit Flyer out into the bright June sunlight and hopped on. She rolled down the driveway and turned toward the downtown section of Centerville. John followed her, pedaling fast to catch up.

Rolling along, the big balloon tires sang over the street as the cool Monday morning breeze washed their faces. But even the refreshing breeze couldn't wash away the nagging doubts that Susan felt. She gripped the handlebars of the old red bicycle harder, and hoped she wasn't making a big mistake.

THROUGH
THE BLACK
WINDOW

· · · · · · · ·

2

The trip downtown seemed longer than usual to Susan because she kept wondering if she was doing the right thing. Centerville was built around a town square. Main Street ran into the square on the south end and continued on out the north end. All the numbered streets ran east and west while the streets with names like Elm and Maple ran north and south like Main. Most of the businesses in town faced the square or were on Main Street. A small shopping center was being built just outside of town near the four-lane highway, but it hadn't opened yet. Most of the gas stations and restaurants were out by the highway too.

The county courthouse, the biggest building in town, was located in the center of the square. The rest of the square was like a park, with grass and trees and bushes and lots of old wooden rail benches. An ancient wooden bandstand stood near the courthouse on the southeast corner. Through the years a lot of the townspeople in Centerville had wanted to tear down the old bandstand, saying it was outdated and dangerous. Yet more people wanted it to stay. Even so, there was usually only one short band concert a year, which took place on the Fourth of July. Susan liked the old bandstand because she often read library books there under the shade of the gazebo-style roof. As Susan rode past it, she suddenly wished she was reading a good book instead of going on John's snooping mission.

Thinking of reading made Susan think of her new glasses, which she had left at home on purpose. She squinted as she rode because she was slightly nearsighted. Though Susan had simple good looks with her brown hair and brown eyes, she thought that her glasses made her look too serious. John had called her "super serious and sensible Susan" the day she'd come back from the optometrist's office. Though her parents had made John stop calling her that, Susan secretly worried that her glasses did make her appear too solemn.

Susan was slightly taller than John, and quite strong. She had come in third in the softball throw the last two years in her class, over all the boys and girls. She was also a fairly fast runner at long distances. John was a good athlete too. He was especially good at sprinting, like the fifty- and hundred-yard dash. John had straight sandy-blond hair and deep green eyes. Even though John was a cousin, there was a strong Kramar resemblance between Susan and John since his father had looked a lot like Susan's father. Susan thought her father was handsome, though his nose was just a bit long. Even that, she thought, gave him a strong face. As the sheriff for the town of Centerville, she thought he needed a strong face.

The toy store was located on the first block south of the square on

Main Street. A shoe store, hardware store and a beauty parlor were on the same side of the block. The two children rode past the front of the toy store three times. The sign was still in the window and the black curtains still hid everything from sight.

John pedaled around the block to the alley with Susan close behind. John looked behind them, then rode down the narrow alley. Susan sighed, then reluctantly followed her cousin. He stopped when he reached the big garbage container behind the toy store. The garbage bin was a huge metal box on wheels. The little window he wanted to spy in was directly above the trash bin. Six black bars guarded the glass.

"I'll climb up on the garbage bin," John said. "If I stand on the edge, I can reach the window, pull myself up and look inside."

"I think this whole idea is crazy," Susan said. "I mean, what do you expect to see?"

"I'm not sure," John said. "If I don't see anything, maybe there will be something in the garbage. You can tell a lot about a person by their trash. Detectives look at trash all the time."

"I have a bad feeling about this whole scheme," Susan said, looking behind her down the alley. She rocked back and forth on her bicycle. That's when she heard a horn blow. It lasted two seconds, then stopped.

"Who's blowing a horn?" Susan asked, looking around.

"I didn't hear a horn," John said. He stopped and listened.

Then Susan heard the horn blast again. The sound wasn't loud, yet it didn't really seem far away. She had never heard a horn quite like it before.

"You heard it that time, didn't you?" Susan asked.

"You must be hearing things."

"How could you not have heard it? It sounded like it was right here."

John wasn't listening. He looked at the trash bin and got off his Spirit Flyer.

"If this whole thing has something to do with Spirit Flyers or the Deeper World, maybe you shouldn't get off your bike," Susan said.

"Then how could I look in the window?" John asked.

Susan was about to tell him how, but John was already on the top edge of the trash bin. He leaned against the brick wall of the store and sidestepped closer to the window. John paused to look down into the trash bin to see what was inside. The boy frowned.

A large dark object that looked something like a window rested on top of the rest of the trash. Yet this was no ordinary window, if it was a window at all. A black frame, about three feet wide and four feet long, held a single pane of something hard and shiny that looked like black glass.

"Maybe it's plastic," John mumbled. "But who could see through that?"

"What's plastic?"

John ignored his cousin's question. The boy began to feel afraid. Something about the black window seemed vaguely familiar. He leaned over and looked closer. Suddenly, the blackness quivered like water on the surface of a pond. John could almost see through the darkness, as if looking through deep shadowy water. As he looked deeper, a blurry image began to appear as if rising up out of the darkness. Then the image finally came to the surface.

John gasped as he saw his own reflection staring back at him. But this was a different kind of reflection. The person in the black window had a dark chain wrapped around his neck. The ends of the chain seemed to be coming right up out of the glass toward John. As the hands in the reflection moved up and touched the chain, John realized his own hands were moving in the same way. John looked down at himself and realized he was touching something cold and hard, but invisible.

At that moment, the reflection of John in the black window grinned and yanked on the chain. John yelled as he lost his balance and he fell face down toward the grinning face. John screamed, but the scream was swallowed by the sound of a splash.

"John?" Susan called. "John, are you all right?"

Susan listened. Without thinking, she jumped off her Spirit Flyer and climbed quickly up the side of the trash bin. John was nowhere in sight. A strange black windowlike object was lying on top of swirls of paper and the other trash.

"John, where are you?" Susan asked. She looked carefully around in the trash bin. "John?"

The shiny surface of the black window quivered slightly like water. Susan climbed over the edge of the metal container and dropped down. The trash came up to her knees.

"John? Where are you?" Susan asked. The black shiny panel moved again. Susan shuffled forward and looked down at it. She rubbed her eyes. Far away, deep inside the window she thought she saw something move as if she were looking down into deep water. As she strained to see, a face floated up toward Susan out of the darkness. She gasped when she recognized who it was.

"John!" she called. Without thinking she reached toward him. But just as she reached forward, she heard the same sound of a blowing horn that she had heard before. She cocked her head for moment, trying to determine where the sound was coming from. She frowned and shrugged her shoulders. Then she reached out slowly and touched the surface of the black window.

The instant she touched it, her hand was sucked in with a swoosh, and almost as fast, her whole body had gone through. Everything went dark in the blink of an eye. All she heard was a blaring horn, a rattling chain and a tiny splash.

Susan barely had time to scream before she heard a sound like a cork popping out of a bottle. Suddenly there was daylight. She looked in front of her and gasped at what she saw. John was standing before her about fifteen feet away. But not only John. Another person that looked just like John was standing beside the first John.

"John, I'm seeing double," Susan said. She rubbed her eyes. When she opened them again, there were still two Johns. One John looked different though, somewhat pale and almost two dimensional, more like a photograph or a ghost than the real person. The ghostly John seemed to be looking at the other John and pulling on something invisible.

"Two of me? You mean you see him?" the solid John asked with a horrified expression on his face. Then the ghostly thin face of the other John looked at Susan and smiled. The real John opened his mouth to scream. "Noooooooooo!"

As Susan rubbed her eyes, the ghostly thin John stuck his tongue out at Susan, then took a short step and faded right into the solid John.

"No. It can't be," John said, shaking his head with his eyes closed. "Not again. I got away this time."

"It's ok, I only see one of you," Susan said.

The boy stopped shaking his head and looked at his cousin.

"I'm normal?" he asked.

"Yes," Susan said. Then she thought. "I mean, I guess so."

Susan looked around. She was in a long dug-out hole. John had just come out of the same hole himself and was looking around when Susan appeared.

"What happened?" Susan asked, looking up at John. The hole was almost waist deep. They were no longer in the alley, and there was no sign of the trash bin. She looked down. Her feet were standing on a shiny black object that looked exactly like the dark window in the trash bin. Only this time it seemed hard, like glass, since she didn't fall through it as she stood on it. Susan hopped off the odd window, then looked around once more.

Garbage surrounded her in the distance like small mountains. That's when she noticed the awful smell. The hole she was standing in was about fifteen feet wide and twenty feet long. And that hole was in a deeper dug-out area that was about the size of a baseball diamond.

She pulled herself out of the hole and dusted off her hands and the knees of her blue jeans.

"I felt as if I got sucked through a vacuum cleaner," Susan said. "I thought I saw you inside that black window. When I reached out for you, I was sucked through. It seemed almost like water that wasn't wet, yet it wasn't like air either. I didn't even have time to think about it, I was here so fast. A swish and a pop, and here we are. But where are we?"

"Don't you know anything? This is the Centerville dump," John said. "Roger and I come out sometimes. Mr. Braker, the dump man, digs out a new pit every so often and they fill it up with garbage. When it's full, they cover the pit up with dirt. The Spirit Flyer was in a mound over there when I first saw it. But he's covered that whole area up."

Susan turned around to see where John was looking. A whole section of the dump was covered with fresh bare dirt with bulldozer tracks crisscrossing over it.

Susan looked back at John. He was peeping down over the edge of the hole as if he were afraid to look into the black window.

"I wouldn't get close to that if I were you," Susan said.

"It seems like any ordinary hole," John said. "Except for that black window thing. You say you came straight through? You didn't stop . . . anyplace?"

"It was like a flash or the blink of an eye," Susan said, frowning. She pulled her long brown hair out of her face. She looked down at her watch. "I wasn't checking, but I don't think much time has passed. It all happened so fast."

"Oh," John said softly. Susan stared at him. He seemed dirty, or different. His blue jeans and T-shirt were more messed up than her clothes.

"Did you come straight through?" Susan asked. "Or did it seem longer?"

John didn't answer. He opened his hands and saw a dark gray powder on them. He started to say something, then stopped.

"What's that stuff?" Susan asked.

"Ashes," John said. "But a few seconds ago it was a . . ."

Susan watched him carefully. John rubbed his hands together to get rid of the ashes. Then he slapped his clothes and small clouds of black sooty smoke surrounded the boy. John looked at the dark puffs in surprise. Then he felt around his neck carefully for a moment.

"Where did you go, John?" Susan asked. "Did you go to the same place that you disappeared to before?"

"Why do you keep bringing that up?" John asked irritably. "I didn't know any of this was going to happen. They said I could keep the toys."

"What toys?" Susan asked. She stared at her cousin. His face was full of confusion. "What are you talking about?"

"I didn't have a chance," John moaned. "I lost my balance because that chain . . ."

John suddenly stopped speaking and his mouth fell open. Susan stared at him. He didn't seem to notice her since he was looking back toward the hole in the pit. A look of terror crossed his face. Then without a word, he turned around and began to run.

"What chain?" Susan asked. But John kept running. Susan looked back, yet didn't see what frightened the boy. She ran after him, calling his name, but John wouldn't stop running. He looked over his shoulder once, as if someone or something was chasing him. Though he seemed to be looking right at something, Susan was sure it wasn't her. He ran past the gate that led out onto the old dump road and headed toward town. By the time Susan reached the dirt road, John was a hundred yards ahead of her and still running as if a ghost were after him.

In another part of the dump, an old woman peeked from behind a mound of trash, watching the boy and girl as they ran away. She had a pleasant smile on her face. She was a small tidy woman, with her gray hair combed in a neat bun. A long black snake was coiled in her arms. The old woman stroked its shiny back as if it were a kitten. The snake's head rose in the air and spread its hood like a cobra. On the throat of the snake was a curious marking: a white X in the center was inside a white circle. The snake watched the children also. It flicked out a blood red tongue and hissed.

26

"Don't be too eager," the woman said. "We must do this carefully this time. And completely. They said there'd be more of those bicycles. All it takes is time though, just a little time and a few toys."

The snake hissed again, the red eyes staring after the children. Like a flash of black lightning, it struck down and bit the woman's arm. Smoke curled up from its jaws as the fangs held tight. The old woman jerked her arm, but more as reflex than out of pain.

"If you insist," the woman sneered. "But remember, I'm only following orders. If you had done your job correctly in the first place, we wouldn't be on this assignment. Why the Bureau sticks me with an amateur like you is more than an insult."

The snake released its hold on the old woman's arm. As the fangs retracted, a puff of smoke came up out of the two dark holes, but no blood. She flung the snake up into the air. The black body wiggled and waggled against the blue sky and kept going higher and higher. Then the wiggling began to look like flapping wings because that's what it was—the wings of a black crow. The crow flew up, then dove down, landing on the woman's outstretched arm.

"The trial run is complete," said the woman with a bored expression. "This may be easier than we thought, but then I'm going strictly by the manual as you should have done. It's all in the chapter called 'Fear and Desire.' You feed their greed and their fears and you control the person. Elementary procedures except for a birdbrain like you. We'll have all the children eating ashes on the target day, you'll see. The Fourth of July is on its way. And on Independence Day when the fireworks start, I'll get signatures on the dotted line and *in blood* like the manual says. You just wait. The Bureau knows I get results. Then I'll get promoted back into a *real* job in one of the bigger cities. I'll have all the ashes I want and a host of fools to feed me."

"The girl?" the crow croaked in a reedy small voice. "What about the girl?"

"We'll get to her," the old woman said confidently. "Just like her cousin. Her bicycle has the instruments attached, but she seems ignorant of how to use them. Fortunately, we made a deal with the boy about his instruments. He can't wait to get the toys. But a little tug of the chain keeps him off balance. Did you see the little fool run? You have to keep their fear hot and sticky. Greed and fear are the best glue to repair a broken chain. But there are a thousand other ways to keep the Order of the Chains too. If you had read your manual, you would know that. But no, you had to botch an X-Removal Plan and let the boy in with his bicycle so they all escaped. Now we've got a bigger mess than the one you started with. That's why you're the birdbrain and I'm in command. The girl will be a tough one to crack. But as long as we follow standard procedures we'll fix her chain soon enough, and with her cooperation. Now, go and follow them."

The crow bobbed up and down obediently, then flew off into the sky. He circled over the dump, then headed toward town.

The old woman chuckled softly to herself as she watched the crow. Then she walked carefully through the mounds of trash down to the newly dug pit. She raised her arms and the shiny black window floated up out of the hole. As she walked toward it, the black window moved to her. The woman stepped into the panel of darkness as if she were walking through a door. The blackness rippled like oil as it sucked her in without a sound. Then the window shrunk to a dot and was gone.

THE COBRA
CLUB
LISTENS IN
· · · · · · · · ·

3

Back in the alley behind the toy store, the abandoned Spirit Flyer bicycles had been discovered. A gang of boys rocked back and forth on black ten-speed bikes, talking about their find. Right below the handlebars on each bike was the picture of a cobra, ready to strike. There were seven boys but only six bicycles. The biggest boy was on foot.

"What do you think we should do, Barry?" Doug Barns asked the boy without a bike.

"I'm thinking," Barry Smedlowe said. He looked at the two Spirit Flyers closely. "I thought there was only one of those ugly old bikes."

"I think there's more than that," Alvin said. "I saw all of those Kramars out riding one evening a few weeks ago. Even Sheriff Kramar had one. But what difference does that make?"

"I'm not sure," Barry replied.

"Why don't you take one, until you get new tires for your bike?" Alvin asked. Barry shook his head quickly.

"I wouldn't be caught dead on one of those fat, ugly bikes," Barry said and grunted.

"Yeah," Robert said laughing. The other boys laughed too, except Barry.

"But they belong to Susan and John Kramar, and aren't they enemies of the club?" Doug asked. "We need to do something."

Barry made a fist and nodded. He had a long-standing grudge against the Kramar kids. When Barry formed the Cobra Club right after Christmas, John Kramar was the first person Barry had asked to join. But John had refused, knowing that Barry would just boss everyone around. John had even kidded the club members, calling them the Dead Men's Club because they sometimes wore black pants and black jackets with the emblem of a cobra's head on the back.

There were some advantages to being in the Cobra Club. Barry's parents wanted him to have lots of friends, so they tended to give him whatever he wanted for the club meetings. And when the club members occasionally caused trouble, Barry was a master at keeping them from getting caught, even when he had tried to steal John's Spirit Flyer. But Barry had found out the hard way that stealing a magic bicycle like the Spirit Flyer wasn't easy. The whole plan had backfired and been like a nightmare to him. He knew the old bikes had some kind of mysterious power, but he didn't know how they worked. So this time as he looked at the two red bicycles, he was determined to be more careful.

"What do you want to do if you don't want to take them?" Doug asked.

"We need to do something since those Kramars are official enemies of the Club," Barry said. Then he looked up and down the alley. "But

this may be some kind of trick to get us in trouble. I mean, why would they just leave their bikes here? Our clubhouse is just down the alley. Maybe they were here, spying."

"But they don't know that's our clubhouse," Freddie said. The clubhouse was an abandoned wooden shed behind the hardware store. "And none of us went in while you were on vacation. That would have broken the oath."

The other boys nodded seriously, remembering the night they had joined the club. Each of them had dripped a drop of their own blood into the flame of a candle and were sworn to many secrets. An awful punishment waited for anyone who broke the oath.

"What should we do with the bikes, though?" Doug asked. Barry looked at the trash bin and then smiled.

"What does anyone do with trash?" Barry asked. "You throw it away."

Barry patted the side of the garbage container. The other boys began grinning and looking at the trash bin.

"In fact, you know, maybe they left these bikes here to be hauled off by the garbage collectors," Barry said. "Anyone would think they look like trash. Maybe we should just help the garbage men out. As trash, they're a nuisance. Someone might trip and fall over these bicycles. Or they might get run over by a car. That would be so sad."

The other boys howled with laughter and grinned like goons.

"Let's dump them in the trash bin," Doug said.

"Yeah," Robert nodded. "Trash for the junk pile."

"Wait," Doug said. "I see someone coming, way down the alley. See?"

Doug pointed. Everyone looked. Two children were walking toward them.

"I bet that's those Kramars," Barry said, squinting. "Quick, into the clubhouse. They won't see us if we go in the back entrance. Maybe we can find out what's going on."

The boys moved quickly to the side of the alley. By the time Susan and John arrived, the Cobra Club was safely hidden in the clubhouse.

Susan and John hadn't seen the boys go into the old shed, though they had seen them running away.

"I don't think they did anything," John said as he ran up to his Spirit Flyer. He bent down to examine the old red bicycle carefully. "We must have scared them off."

"It doesn't take much to scare those boys," Susan said, checking out her bicycle. "They're only brave if it's seven against one."

"Yeah," John said. "But it's really you that they're afraid of."

Susan smiled. John seemed to be acting like himself again, at least for a while.

Susan had run after him all the way down the dump road. John had finally stopped when he got to the Sleepy Eye River. He had waited for her at the bridge, yet refused to talk about his behavior at the dump as they walked back into town on Crofts Road. Susan felt quite certain that their journey through the black window was somehow connected to the time John disappeared three weeks before. Yet the more Susan had questioned him, the more stubborn John had seemed in his silence. Susan had finally given up trying though she was quite frustrated deep inside about the morning's unusual adventure.

Now John's face was serious. He climbed up the side of the trash bin and carefully looked over the edge.

"There's nothing but trash," he said, sounding relieved. The boy felt around his neck for a moment. When he saw Susan looking at him, he quickly stopped. "That black window thing is gone. Everything seems back to normal."

"What's normal?" Susan asked. She climbed up beside John and looked in the trash bin too.

"That's what I'd like to know," John replied.

"I think we should tell Dad," Susan said. Both children hopped down.

"Tell him what?" John asked. "There's nothing to show him here. The window is gone. The one out at the dump might still be there. But since we didn't really get hurt or anything, I don't think we should tell Not unless we find out something definite. You know how he is. He didn't believe me the first time I told him about my Spirit Flyer. Why should he believe this?"

"But that was before we all got Spirit Flyers," Susan said. "He might believe us now. He knows they're different. And that deeper things can happen."

"Yeah, but he doesn't like it very much," John said. "He hardly ever rides his Spirit Flyer, not even around town like a regular bicycle."

"I don't think Dad's gotten used to the idea," Susan said. "Some people just don't change very fast. Besides, you haven't ridden your Spirit Flyer much either these last few weeks."

"Well, I have my reasons," John said and frowned. He looked at the trash bin, and once more felt at his neck. This time he didn't seem to notice that Susan was watching.

John picked up his heavy red bicycle and leaned it against his leg. He looked it over carefully.

"At least Barry and the Dead Men's Club didn't do any damage," John said. "I didn't know he was back in town. I was hoping he'd stay away on vacation all summer."

"And all fall," Susan added and laughed. Then her face got serious. "At the dump you said something about 'keeping the toys.' What did you mean? Did you see some toys at the dump?"

"Did you see them too?" John asked mysteriously. Then he frowned. "They belong to me, every one of them. I made a . . ." Then the boy went silent, as if he had said too much. Before Susan could ask another question, John hopped on his bicycle and rode down the alley.

"Wait up," Susan called and pedaled after her cousin. "We need to go mow lawns."

When they were sure John and Susan had gone, the Cobra Club filed out of the old wooden shed. Barry beat his fist into the palm of his hand.

"We need to do something about John Kramar and that brat sister of his, and I mean soon," Barry said, his face tight with fury. "Dead Men's

Club. Bah! We'll fix them both."

"But how?" Doug asked. "And what do you suppose they were talking about? A black window thing and the dump?"

"Yeah," Alvin added. "They said something about toys at the dump too. He was acting funny, like it was a big secret."

The bigger boy's eyes brightened. He began to grin.

"Maybe so," Barry said. "But if they're looking for toys, they won't keep them. Because we'll be right behind them, all the way. Ever since John Kramar got that junky old bicycle, strange things have been going on. And now his whole dopey family has Spirit Flyers."

"Yeah," the other boys grumbled.

"We need to keep our eyes on Susan and John," Barry said. "We'll keep a watch on their house and tail them. Let me tell you how it will go. This will be our first assignment for the summer."

The boys followed Barry back into the old wooden shed and huddled around to hear the big boy's plan.

SUSAN'S INCREDIBLE TALE

· · · · · · · · ·

4

Later that afternoon Susan and John argued all the way to the sheriff's office about whether to tell about their adventure at the dump. They were both so wrapped up in their fight that they didn't notice the boys from the Cobra Club following them from a distance.

The sheriff's office in Centerville was located on the corner of Maple and Tenth Street, a few blocks west from the town square. For years, the entire police department had been in the big courthouse building. But when a new factory had opened up on the edge of town thirty years before, the town had grown. The town council had moved the sheriff's office into a new, more modern building with more room and better facilities.

Susan knocked down the kickstand and parked her Spirit Flyer by the front steps to the sheriff's office. John practically dropped his bike down on the sidewalk and scrambled up the steps past her. He stopped in front of the door, blocking her way.

"Just wait and think," John said.

"I've already made up my mind," Susan snapped back. "I think we should tell Dad and I'm going to do it. Now move out of my way."

"Will you just wait a second?" John asked, holding his hands up like a crossing guard at school. "Just because you read a few pages of an old book about Spirit Flyers doesn't mean you're suddenly an expert. After all, I've had my Spirit Flyer a lot longer than you. Don't forget that I was the one who caught those thieves who . . ."

"You've been saying that all afternoon," Susan sneered impatiently. "But you don't really know what's going on any more than I do. I think you're just scared. In fact, I think something happened when you disappeared, and you don't want us to know for some reason."

"What have I got to hide?" John said in his most innocent voice.

"I wonder," Susan snapped.

As they worked cutting grass that day, she had decided that she would tell her father what had happened. John was completely against the idea. First he begged her not to tell, and then he almost threatened her if she did tell. She was convinced he was either hiding something or just blind to the strange way he was behaving. But besides being upset, deep down she was also somewhat worried about her cousin.

"If you tell him what happened, we'll probably get in trouble and he won't want us to investigate anymore," John whined. "Something important may be about to happen and I need to be free to get around."

"What do you mean?" Susan asked. "What do you think is going to happen?"

"I'm not really at liberty to say," John said with a note of superiority in his voice. "These things are complicated and since you've only had your Spirit Flyer for a short time, unlike me, you probably wouldn't understand anyway. When you've proven yourself worthy, the way I did when I brought back all those . . ."

"Out of my way, you pompous windbag," Susan said, and pushed him off balance. She opened the door and darted inside before John could stop her.

"Wait," John yelled as he rushed in after her.

"Wait for what?" George the deputy asked. He rolled his wheelchair over to the long front counter of the sheriff's office and stared at the two children.

Susan ignored the deputy and walked past the front counter with John hot on her heels. She opened her father's office door without knocking and went in. John slammed the door shut.

Sheriff Kramar hardly had a chance to say hello. Susan quickly blurted out the whole story about the black window behind the toy store and at the dump. And when she was finished with that, she complained about John's behavior in general, and then in a list of specific details. John tried to interrupt a few times, but Susan kept talking. Sheriff Kramar's face grew more and more serious as he listened.

Susan sighed when she finally finished. Then she looked at John and smiled with great satisfaction, as if daring him to speak. Sheriff Kramar looked at both children. His face looked tired. He had been working longer hours than usual since one of his deputies was on vacation. And besides that, Mrs. Kramar had been sick in bed the last week.

"What's your side of this somewhat incredible tale?" Sheriff Kramar asked John.

"Why are you calling it a 'tale' as if it's a story or something?" Susan blurted out defensively. "You act like I've made everything up."

" 'Incredible tale' were his actual words," John said. He smiled sweetly at Susan and stuck his tongue out when Sheriff Kramar wasn't looking.

"Now he's sticking out his tongue," Susan complained. "How juvenile. And you think you're so experienced and everything."

John quickly sucked his tongue inside before his uncle could see. While Susan was talking, he smiled to himself. A brilliant idea had come to the boy as if out of nowhere. Though he knew such a plan was risky, he decided it was worth it under the circumstances. "Once I get the toys, then I can make it up to her," the boy thought to himself.

"Susan is imagining things, Uncle Bill," John blurted out. "I think she got heat stroke cutting the grass with me today. I tried to tell her to calm down, but she wouldn't. We were at the toy store and dump this morning, but we were just looking around."

Susan dropped her jaw in surprise. She knew John had not been his usual self lately, but she had never known him to lie. She stared at her cousin in surprise, utterly speechless, but only for a moment.

"Why you little . . ."

"Hold it right there," Sheriff Kramar said firmly. "The best way I know to examine a story is to examine the evidence. Let's just swing by the toy store and dump on our way home to supper."

"But we told you the black window thing in the trash can was gone by the time we got back," Susan protested.

"You said there was one out at the dump though," John said.

"What do you mean, 'I said,' as if you didn't see it too?" Susan accused. "You're trying to make me look like I made the whole thing up. You know what happened. I can't believe it."

"Let's just go take a look," Sheriff Kramar replied with a tired voice. He stood up and moved toward the door.

Susan protested all the way to her father's police car. John winked at George on their way out the door. Then he smiled with satisfaction at Susan which only made her rage all the more.

Sheriff Kramar stopped the car in the alley behind the toy store. He stepped up and looked in the big trash bin. Susan scrambled up to look also. The trash bin was empty. Not even a scrap of paper was inside.

"This doesn't prove it wasn't here this morning," Susan said. "Tell him, John. Tell him what really happened."

"I like your version better," John said. "I think it's more entertaining than television, if you ask me."

Susan yelped and went at John with both fists flying. Only the strong arms of her father caught the blows before they ever landed.

"Susan!" he snapped and shook her. Susan struggled, then stopped. For a moment she was ready to burst into tears.

"I won't give him the satisfaction," she thought to herself as she glared at John. Without a word, she crawled into the back seat of the police car and slammed the door.

She sulked all the way to the dump while John talked to her father about baseball teams, something Susan had no interest in whatsoever.

"He's just avoiding the subject," Susan thought. "But he'll have some explaining to do once we get to the dump."

Sheriff Kramar drove slowly into the dumping area.

"Over there," Susan instructed. She looked triumphantly at John. "There's the pit we were in earlier this morning."

Sheriff Kramar rode over to the pit. Susan opened the door before the car stopped. A crow swooped down, gliding over the dump, but none of the Kramars noticed. Susan ran to the long pit. John held back, a nervous expression on his face.

"It's right in this hole," Susan said as she ran up to the edge. But the hole was empty. Susan made her hands into fists, then stomped her foot. Sheriff Kramar and John walked over.

"I don't see anything," Sheriff Kramar said.

"Neither do I," John said, a big smile breaking out across his face.

"I'm telling you it was there," Susan said. "Just because it's gone now, doesn't mean it wasn't there."

Sheriff Kramar nodded. He looked down at the ground.

"I don't understand," she said.

"Well, you weren't wearing your glasses today like you should have been," John said condescendingly. "So who knows what a half-blind person like you could have . . ."

"That's enough!" Sheriff Kramar said when he saw Susan going for John. Susan clenched her fists and stopped, but tears quickly filled her eyes. She turned her back on them so John wouldn't see her cry. She wiped her eyes with the back of her hand.

Sheriff Kramar looked around the dump. The black crow had landed on top of a mound of trash and was perched on an old chair, staring at them.

"Let's go home and eat," the sheriff said. He put his arm around Susan. "And I want you two to quit fighting. I've never seen you both act so mean to one another."

"She's just upset over some boy or something," John said.

"I am not!" Susan said shrilly. "You are . . . you are . . . the biggest liar that . . ."

Then she went silent, knowing she would get in more trouble if she said what she felt. Her father had strict rules about name calling and he enforced those rules to the letter. Susan had rarely gotten in trouble as John often did, but today she felt as if the tables were turned.

"I think you need to apologize to John right now," her father said sternly. Susan looked down avoiding his stare. She waited and waited.

"I'm sorry I called you a name," she mumbled. "But what I said about those black window things is true, I'm telling you. Why would I make up something like that?"

"That's what I would like to know," John said. "Normally, you're so serious and sensible. You should go on TV and . . ."

"John, you keep quiet," Sheriff Kramar said. "Let's just cool off and go home."

No one spoke on the way back to town. Susan and John got off at the sheriff's office to get their bikes. Sheriff Kramar drove on.

Susan groaned when she saw her bike. Both of the big balloon tires were squashed flat.

"It figures," she said to herself. She jerked the old bicycle, kicked viciously at the kickstand and began pushing the Spirit Flyer home, seething inside as she went. She had already decided in the car that she was never going to speak to John again for the rest of her whole life.

The tires on John's Spirit Flyer were flat too, but he hardly seemed to notice. He pushed his bike after Susan, but kept his distance.

"What's wrong with Susan and John?" Katherine asked. She was five years old and the youngest in the Kramar family. Everyone was home getting ready for supper.

"They had a fight," Lois said cheerfully, as she set out the silverware for the table. Lois was seven and very precise. She made sure the forks and knives and spoons were in the exact right places. "Susan called John a liar and got in trouble."

"She's grouchy," Katherine said in her small voice. She skipped into the kitchen to get the napkins and put them in the napkin rings. That was her job. Susan was stirring a pan full of spaghetti sauce on the stove.

Susan cooked that evening since her mother was sick. Her mother didn't even come to the table. Mrs. Kramar had been sick on and off all week, but none of the children knew what kind of sickness it was. She didn't seem to have a cold or anything contagious. And she wasn't taking any medicine even. The children were puzzled by the whole thing.

Susan was more than ready for her mother to get well. As the oldest child, Susan always had more chores to do around the house if her mother was sick. She didn't think it was fair. John didn't have to help as much, she thought, which made Susan feel even more bitter about the day's events. She would have refused John's help even if he had offered since she was determined not to speak to him. Life was just unfair, no question about it. And to make things worse, she burned herself when the bubbling spaghetti sauce spattered up on her hand.

Susan was the last to sit down for supper. The table seemed out of balance without her mother in her usual place. Her father talked about a new company that was coming to Centerville to use the old factory on the outside of town. The factory had been closed and empty for several years. But Susan didn't care about such news. She asked to be excused after she ate a few hurried bites. She stared hard at John once before she left, then went to her room.

She pulled *The Book of the Kings* off her bookshelf and opened it. She reluctantly put on her glasses. Soon she was turning the old worn pages with increasing speed. She had already read some of the same parts before, but she felt like she needed something to explain the odd events of the day. Susan was convinced John's obnoxious behavior about the strange black window had something to do with the workings of the Deeper World.

The Book of the Kings told stories full of Magic and wonder from beginning to end. Yet it was also a book filled with many sorrows as it told of the lives lost to Treason's deadly domain. Even places like the small town of Centerville were under the tragic shadow of Treason and his band of rebels.

Susan had read enough of the book to know that even ordinary people were somehow in the middle of this continuing deeper battle. And deep inside, she wondered if John Kramar could have been affected some way when he disappeared. John had his faults, but to lie the way he had seemed bizarre to Susan.

Before he had left, Grandfather Kramar had spoken of the tragic powers of the Deeper Chains. Susan didn't know much about these mysterious chains, except that they were dangerous. She wondered if John's strange behavior was connected to the chains somehow, as if he were under a spell. The girl didn't know that there were certain deep secrets that could only be discovered; you had to do more than just read about them in the book.

But without the book, nothing in the world made much sense. Susan believed that if John would only read *The Book of the Kings,* he might find the doorway to the help he needed. But John seemed to be preoccupied with the toy store and some terrible secret inside.

Susan put the big book on a shelf and turned out the light. She opened her window to look out at the night stars, but the sky was dark with clouds. The world seemed so lonely and unfair to the girl. If there was a battle going on in the shadows, Susan felt that the darkness must be winning. She fell into a restless sleep of bad dreams that she would forget before waking.

MRS. HAPPY
BUYS
A STORE
· · · · · · · ·

5

The next morning at the Centerville Toy Store, the front door was still locked. Mr. Potter, the owner, was inside talking to a little old woman with white hair. His face was red and sweating. He looked down at a briefcase full of money.

"I still don't understand why you would pay so much for my store, Mrs. . . ."

"Happy," the woman said, a twinkle in her eye.

"Right, Mrs. Happy," Mr. Potter said. "I mean, we make money, but the store really isn't worth *this* much."

"Worth means different things to different people, Mr. Potter. My late husband and I loved children, though we never had any of our own. On his deathbed, he urged me to use part of the fortune we'd made during our lifetime to make children happy. And what could make them more happy than toys?"

"But why Centerville, and why so quickly?" Mr. Potter asked. "I mean, there are other towns, bigger towns, where toy stores make more money."

"Yes, I suppose that's so," Mrs. Happy said, her blue eyes twinkling. "But Centerville has a strong attraction to me. I've been watching the children here and I know I can do a good job on them . . . I mean, for them. Besides, Centerville is a lovely little town. A town where folks can get to know one another, I would imagine."

"No friendlier folks around than the ones in Centerville, all right," Mr. Potter agreed, nodding his head. "Still, this is so much money."

"I could always open another toy store," Mrs. Happy said. Her smile froze. "If you want the competition? In that case, I could just withdraw my offer as quickly as I made it."

"No problem, really, Mrs. Happy," Mr. Potter said, closing the briefcase. "The paperwork's all done. We can go over to the barbershop and get Ike to notarize it. This includes the toy store and that land by the cemetery. Why you'd want to buy that old field is another thing. No one will ever want to live out there. The cemetery's already got plenty of space so the town won't want to buy it. The only other thing nearby is the old factory and it's been closed up for several years now. Are you sure you want that property too?"

"Of course," Mrs. Happy said.

"But why?" Mr. Potter asked. He wiped his upper lip with the back of his hand.

"I think it's a pretty field. Besides, I might want room to expand," Mrs. Happy replied. "Expansion is important to me."

"If you say so," Mr. Potter said. He rubbed his head and looked down at the legal papers in his hands. "I think everything's in order."

"Oh, there is one other condition, a very tiny one," the old woman said.

"What?" asked Mr. Potter, puzzled.

"If anyone asks, you are to refer to me as a distant cousin, a relative."

"But you aren't related to me," Mr. Potter replied. "Why would you want me to tell a silly lie like that?"

"I have my reasons. One is that it is better for business. And if you want the extra high price you are getting for your store and land, you will do as I say."

She stared at Mr. Potter, the twinkle gone from her eyes. He swallowed uncomfortably.

"Look at all that money," the old woman said. She ran her hand over the stacks of cash wrapped in neat packets. "No more questions, please. That's part of the deal."

Mr. Potter rubbed his finger over his lip. "If it's that important, I guess I could fib a little," Mr. Potter said. "But remember, I'm an honest man."

"Aren't you all," she said and smiled once more. "Shall we go, then?"

Mrs. Happy walked to the front door and waited. Mr. Potter rushed after her. He opened the front door.

"After you," she said, the twinkle had returned to her eye. Mr. Potter walked outside. She shut the door behind him.

Five minutes later she returned alone. She locked the front door behind her and walked straight to the rear of the store which served as an office and workshop. She sat down at a worn roll-top desk. She rolled the cover back. With one sweep of her arm, she wiped all the papers and boxes off the desk top onto the floor.

She then reached down into a carpetbag and lifted out a small object that resembled a small picture frame about three inches tall and two inches wide. The frame surrounded a pane of black glass or plastic. She put it on the desk. She closed her eyes, then began to pull. The black frame grew taller and wider. She pulled until it was about three feet tall by two feet wide. She smiled.

She reached into her bag again and pulled out a thin metal rod. The black rod looked like a long knitting needle with a sharp hook on the end. She stared at the black window and waited. In a moment, a blurred image appeared, then came into focus on a boy pushing a bike with two flat tires down a sidewalk. The boy was Barry Smedlowe.

"Just in time, I see," Mrs. Happy said, smiling. She stuck the hook carefully into the window. The hook went through easily. In the picture, Barry suddenly stopped. The old woman smiled.

"Come here, now," Mrs. Happy commanded. She pulled the hook slowly out of the window. She inspected the tip of the hook and then put it in her carpetbag.

She left the window on the desk and walked out of the little office. At the front of the store, she pulled back the black curtains that covered the large display windows. Then she unlocked the door.

Moments later, a large tractor-trailer truck rumbled up in front of the store and stopped. Some men in gray uniforms got out. Mrs. Happy talked with them awhile. The men began carting boxes out of the store, loading them into the trailer.

Mrs. Happy looked at the clock as the men worked quietly. She got out a ball of black yarn and a hook. Her fingers began to crochet as she waited.

Barry Smedlowe had sent two club members to watch the Kramar house that morning. In the meantime, he was hoping to get the tires fixed on his bicycle, a Goliath Cobra Deluxe.

The black ten-speed was a mess. Both tires were totally destroyed, as if they'd been melted. Besides that, a curious black metal box about seven inches square was attached to the handlebars. On the side of the box facing the rider was an odd marking: a white circle with a white X inside. Barry knew there was something unusual about the box. Soon after he had tried to steal John Kramar's Spirit Flyer several weeks before, Barry had had an awful experience which he thought was a nightmare.

When he woke up the next day, the black box was on his bicycle and the tires were melted flat. He knew the box had something to do with his dream, but like many dreams, he couldn't remember it.

Barry was afraid of the box. He had touched it once, and sparks flew off and shocked him. Since then, he had left the bike and box alone.

But being without his bike during summertime was too big a burden on the boy. He decided he would let someone else fix his bike. He got some money and then began pushing his bike downtown to Fenly's filling station.

Barry was sweating by the time he got to Main Street. Pushing the bike with flat tires was hard work. He felt as if he was pushing a truck into town instead of a bicycle.

At the corner, he headed south toward Fenly's filling station and garage. But as soon as he turned the handlebars, the wheels locked. Barry pushed, but the burnt tires seemed to stick to the cement sidewalk like gluey tar.

"Come on, you trash-heap bike," Barry grunted, pushing with all his might. Then he thought of something. The Centerville Toy Store sold tires and tubes for bicycles too. He knew the store had been closed, yet he thought he would take a chance. And when he turned the bike toward the toy store, the tires began to roll easily once more.

"Crazy bike," Barry muttered. "It won't hurt to check."

A big truck was parked in front of the toy store. Barry pushed his bike down the sidewalk. He paused as two men rolled a cart out of the front door, loading a box into the truck. Then men went back inside the toy store. Barry followed them, stopping at the door.

"Come in, young man, I've been waiting for you," said an old woman with white hair and a pleasant face. She smiled at Barry, then looked carefully at the black box stuck to the handlebars of his Goliath Cobra Deluxe.

The bike seemed to roll through the door without Barry even trying to push it.

"Hey, what's going on?" Barry asked suspiciously. "Where's Mr. Potter? I thought the store was closed."

"I'm Mrs. Happy, the new owner of this establishment," Mrs. Happy said cheerfully. "And you are my first customer."

"I am?" Barry asked. He looked around the store. Everything had changed. Half the shelves were empty and two men were busy packing boxes with the toys that were left.

"And to celebrate," Mrs. Happy said. "I'm giving my first customer free merchandise. After all, you are Number One."

"I could use some new tires for my bike," Barry said hopefully.

"Why not throw in some free tubes as well," Mrs. Happy replied. "What good's a tire without a tube on a bicycle?"

"That's right," Barry agreed enthusiastically.

"I'll do even better than that," she said. "Roll your bike to the back of the store and I'll have them put on and pumped up while you wait."

"Really?" Barry asked.

"Follow me," Mrs. Happy said. "But watch out for the workers. They are taking some toys away for processing."

"Processing? What do you mean?" Barry asked.

The old woman didn't seem to hear him. Barry did as he was told, rolling his black Cobra Deluxe to the rear of the store. Mrs. Happy parted a curtain. Barry pushed the bike through.

"Say, can you take that black box off the handlebars too?" Barry asked carefully.

"I thought you'd never ask," Mrs. Happy said with a sense of relief in her voice. "I can do it as long as you are giving me permission."

"Sure, take it," Barry said.

The old woman reached down in her carpetbag and pulled out a piece of paper.

"I'll need you to sign this permission form," Mrs. Happy said, handing the paper to Barry.

"For what?"

"It's a sort of work order, so I can remove the box. It's official business. For my protection, you might say. If you don't sign, I can't work."

Barry started reading the paper, but the print was so fine and so confusing that he gave up. He signed his name by the x on the bottom of the form. Mrs. Happy snatched the paper out of the boy's hand. She stared at the signature and then carefully looked at the black box.

"Your bicycle will be ready soon," she said. "Why don't you have a look around."

While Barry browsed around the toy store, picking things up and then setting them down, Mrs. Happy worked quickly in the back of the store. With a twist and a jerk, she removed the black box from the handlebars. She looked out of the curtain for Barry. He was near the front of the store.

"Only a birdbrain like you would release valuable Bureau property so easily," Mrs. Happy grunted at the crow as she held up the black box. The crow was perched up on top of the desk. "He's a perfect candidate. Too bad you had to mess up everything else with your poor performance on an X-Removal Plan."

"Not my fault, not my fault," the crow squawked.

"At least we'll have this taken care of, not to mention the points I'll earn for recovering it," the old woman said with a smile. She put the box in her carpetbag. "And all for a few measly bicycle tires. I'm going to enjoy using this boy to make the fireworks a big success for me. . . , I mean, for the Bureau. Then you'll see how you get a whole town locked in their chains for good."

A short while later, Mrs. Happy reappeared, pushing the Cobra Deluxe on its shiny new wheels. She had put the new tires and wheels on herself.

"All ready," she said.

"Great," Barry said.

"By the way, I'm planning a big Grand Opening Day Celebration for this Friday, July Fourth," the old woman said. I'll be giving all kinds of good things away. Free toys on the day of freedom. Has a nice ring, doesn't it?"

"Free toys?" Barry asked. He smiled. Then he frowned as he looked at his bike. "Say, do you know what kind of box that was on my handlebars? I thought you might know what it is."

"I do know," she said.

"Well, . . . what is it?" Barry asked.

"I'm not telling," Mrs. Happy said seriously. "I have much to do now, and I don't need little boys underfoot. So be gone."

Barry didn't stand around to argue. She opened the front door and he rolled the Goliath Cobra Deluxe out into the sunshine of the new June day. The door closed with a click.

"A kind of weird old lady," he muttered. "But free is free."

He shook his head, then started pedaling the Goliath Cobra Deluxe down the street. He picked up speed quickly and smiled. The new tires seemed to sing across the pavement.

Barry rounded the corner in high gear. He knew exactly where he wanted to go. A leering grin spread across his face. The big boy pedaled even faster and reached the street where Susan and John Kramar lived in record time.

BARRY
TAILS
JOHN
· · · · · · · ·
6

Susan Kramar was working in the garage that morning when John walked in. The big garage door was open, but neither child noticed Barry Smedlowe ride up and hide behind a tree down the block.

"I'm going to the toy store," John said to Susan. She was leaning over the lawn mower, checking the oil. Susan got an oil can from a garage shelf, then returned to the mower.

Susan was still determined not to speak to John, though she had decided a week of silence would be more practical than forever. She poured the thick oil into the lawn mower as if she hadn't heard John.

"I want to check in the trash container again," John said. "I think you should come with me, maybe."

Susan snorted, then shook her head. She couldn't believe that John had the nerve to ask such a thing. She was tempted to break her silence and tell him what she really thought. But she stubbornly pursed her lips.

"Be that way, then," John complained. He looked at his Spirit Flyer. Seeing the flat tires again just added to his anger. He had tried to pump them up earlier, but all the air leaked out. Deep inside, he figured the bike probably wouldn't work even if he could get the tires pumped up. From past experience, he knew the mysterious old red bicycle had a mind of it's own. For a moment, John considered apologizing to Susan, and trying to make things right. But then the thought of how much trouble he would be in made him stop.

"If my plan works, I can avoid the trouble and still come out ahead," John thought to himself. But John wasn't sure his plan would work.

He wasn't sure of anything, and that was the problem. Nothing had been quite right ever since he had disobeyed his grandfather's instruction on hooking up the gear lever. He hadn't told his family where he had gone the three hours he had disappeared because he was afraid he had made a big mistake on his journey.

John knew that when he had flipped the gear lever, he had shot forward in time somewhere in the Deeper World. On the trip, John had gone to the most exciting place he had ever seen. The old bike had crash-landed right at the foot of a mountain of gleaming toys! Shooting stars had exploded all around him in beautiful colors like fireworks. John had soon realized that the place was high in the air, halfway between the earth and the heavens, directly over Centerville. He had also realized the exploding lights were a display of real fireworks.

John had reached greedily for the first toy when he noticed the chain around his neck. That had been a shock. But what had been more surprising was the ghostly image of a boy that held the other end of the chain. The boy had looked like John himself.

The ghostly boy had been friendly at first. He had promised that John could have the whole mountain of toys if John did one simple thing: not put any of the accessories like the gear lever or light or horn on his Spirit Flyer bicycle. John had resisted at first. But the more the boy talked, the more he had seemed to make sense. He could still keep the bike, John had reasoned with himself. And he would gain a fortune in toys and fun. John had figured that would be more than enough to make up for a bunch of old bicycle instruments, even if they were Magic.

So John had agreed to the deal. But as he picked up the first toy, they all disappeared in a puff and ashes. Then the ghostly boy reminded John that the deal would take place in the future, near the Fourth of July. In the meantime, John had to prove he was serious about keeping his end of the bargain. John began to protest, feeling cheated. That's when things got worse. With the glittering toys gone, John had gotten a better look at his surroundings. John didn't even like to think about what had happened after that. He had felt like he had been trapped in a nightmare. But at the worst moment, he suddenly found himself back home. Three hours had passed in the real world while he had been in the Deeper World.

John had felt ashamed and troubled for weeks. But since he had kept his end of the deal, he still figured he would be collecting the toys any day since the Fourth of July was so close. In fact, when he had gone through the black window behind the toy store, he had seen the toys again. John had been sure that he was finally going to get the toys since he had kept his end of the agreement. But the toys had disappeared again as he picked up the first one. Then John popped through the window again, ending up by the dump.

John figured that it still wasn't the right time. But he was also beginning to have more and more doubts about the deal he had made. He felt torn in two. Part of him wanted to just stop and confess the whole story to his family. Yet the other part of him still hoped to collect the toys. He wanted to go back to the toy store in hopes of finding the black window again. At the same time, he was afraid of what might happen. He had seen something awful in the Deeper World both times, and then he had even seen it at the dump, just for a moment. That's why John wanted Susan to come along, just in case there was trouble.

But she wasn't speaking to him. He didn't blame her, since he had lied the way he had. Still, he was afraid.

He wasn't ready to admit to Susan that he might have made several mistakes. So, without another word, he strode out of the garage toward town. His Spirit Flyer leaned silently against the wall, the two big tires flat as a board.

Susan watched John head down the street. She had been set to go mow and trim the Smither's lawn by herself when she had seen Barry Smedlowe slowly riding down the street. At first she hadn't thought anything of it. But when Barry had pulled behind a tree suddenly, as if hiding, Susan had gotten suspicious. John had just left for the toy store and was two blocks ahead of the bigger boy. When John had stopped at the corner, Barry had stopped. When John had continued walking again, Barry had followed. Susan had watched John and Barry until they were out of sight.

"Who cares?" Susan muttered to herself. "John can take care of himself."

Though she was still feeding off her anger, she felt sad. Deep inside she really loved John very much. As Susan got the clipper and the burlap grass bags, she began to worry. She didn't think Barry would be brave enough to do anything by himself, but if he had his Club, he might try to gang up on John.

Susan kept working. She went inside to take her mother some camomile tea. Mrs. Kramar was reading in bed. Her face was pale. Susan kissed her on the forehead and went back into the garage.

As she was about to drag the lawn mower over to the Smithers, she heard a small horn, just like the noise she had heard the day before. Susan cocked her head, listening carefully.

She looked up and down the street. Then she looked in the garage. The girl's eyes rested on her old red Spirit Flyer. Susan forgot about the sound of the horn when she saw the flat tires. The tires looked so pathetic when they were flat. Susan dragged the mower back inside the garage. Then she got an air pump off the shelf and took it to the front tire of the old red bike. She pumped up the front tire and then the back.

"Maybe I should check on John, just to make sure he's not in any trouble," she said to herself as she put the pump away. In a moment she was rolling down the street toward the center of town.

As John walked he felt worse than ever. He was so deep in his thoughts that he didn't notice Barry Smedlowe carefully following at a distance.

When he got to Main Street, he turned toward the toy store as if pulled by some invisible force. He was surprised to see a large truck and trailer parked in front of the toy store. A ramp led up into the back of the trailer which was filled with cardboard boxes. Men in gray uniforms were pulling the boxes on little handcarts. But he was even more surprised to see Susan waiting for him.

"What are you doing here?" he asked as he walked up to the store.

She wanted to help John but she was still determined not to speak to him. So she just gestured behind John with a nod of her head. Half a block away John saw Barry duck into a doorway as soon as Barry knew he was spotted. Susan had avoided Barry by coming on a side street.

"What's he up to? Has he been following me?" John asked. Susan nodded. "Well, thanks for the warning! You never know what dirty business that Cobra Club may be doing. Why is this truck here? Are they bringing some new toys?" But as the children watched, it became clear that the men were loading the truck, taking toys away.

John and Susan walked up to the front door. A man pushed by him, rolling another big box into the truck.

An old woman with gray hair sat in a rocking chair near the front door. She was crocheting a chain stitch with a long thin hook. A big ball of black yarn was in her lap. She smiled warmly at John, then stared at Susan. Something about the woman's eyes made Susan suspicious right away.

"Hi," John said, stepping through the front door. "Where's Mr. Potter?"

"He's gone," the woman said. "I'm Mrs. Happy, the new owner of this delightful toy store. How can I help you?"

"I just came to look around," John said. He stared at the old woman. Somehow she seemed vaguely familiar to the boy, though he wasn't sure why.

"There's not much to see," Mrs. Happy replied. "Everything's a mess because I'm not really open yet. I have a lot of new toys coming in, but they haven't arrived. In the meantime, I'm clearing out the old toys for processing. When the new toys come in, I'm going to have a Grand Opening Day Celebration this Friday on July Fourth. There will be lots of free toys for all the children in town. I hope you'll come."

"I'll sure be here if there's free toys," John said and smiled eagerly.

"I know you will," the woman replied. Just then, a black crow fluttered across the room from the cash register and landed on Mrs. Happy's shoulder. The little black eyes stared at John.

"How can you afford to give away toys?" Susan asked, finally breaking her silence.

"A new store has to attract new customers," Mrs. Happy said a little too sweetly.

"Seems like a pretty expensive way to get business," Susan said. Somehow Susan knew there was more to Mrs. Happy's plans than what she was saying.

"Some children know how to mind their *own* business," Mrs. Happy said harshly. Then suddenly changing back to her sweet voice, she said, "I just want to create good will with the town of Centerville in the hopes of establishing a long and friendly relationship."

"Hello," the crow said in a squeaky voice. The bird pecked at something in the old woman's hair, then looked back at the two children.

"He talks?" John asked. "I've never seen a talking crow. What's its name?"

"I call him Nail," Mrs. Happy said. "He's a fine bird, though rather careless at times."

"Will you be selling pets when you reopen?" John asked.

"Oh my, no," Mrs. Happy said and laughed. "Nail is just my little helper. I'd ask you to stay, but as you can see, there isn't much to look at. Out with the old and in with the new. That's what I say."

"Out with the old, in with the new," the crow repeated. "Out with the old, and out with you!"

Susan frowned at the crow's odd rhyme. John walked over to an aisle that had held softballs and other sports equipment. Most of the shelves were empty. Another big box was rolled out the door. Mrs. Happy looked out the front window at the sidewalk.

"Most children I've seen are riding bicycles these days," Mrs. Happy said to John. "Are you in need of a good bicycle?"

"No, not really," John said. "My bike has a couple of flat tires right now."

"Is that so?" Mrs. Happy asked. "I may have some new bicycles coming one of these days. Some really special ones. It just depends how well the new line of toys does. They're new and improved, you know. Be sure to come to our Grand Opening Day Celebration. This Friday is the target date. I want everyone to come. Everything will be extra super-wonderful, besides new and improved. And don't miss the fireworks we'll be sponsoring."

"I'll be there for sure," John said.

"We've just got three more boxes to go on the truck," a worker said to Mrs. Happy. He handed her a piece of paper.

"I better go now," John said.

"Good-by, my boy," the old woman said. As Susan started to leave too she added, "You'll come for the free toys too, won't you?"

"I'm not sure," Susan said uncomfortably. There was something she definitely did not trust about this woman or her plan to give away toys. It all sounded too easy.

Susan followed John down the street toward the square, still upset with John but still concerned about him too. He turned and waited for Susan to catch up, and then he kept walking while Susan kept pace on her Spirit Flyer. "Isn't that great about the Grand Opening Celebration and getting free toys?" John asked. "That's the best news I've heard in a long time." Susan remained silent. She couldn't believe that all he had on his mind was toys. "Ok, be that way," John said when she didn't answer. But at least you could have been nice to Mrs. Happy. What do you have against someone who's going to give away toys?"

As they rounded the corner, John saw the alley and remembered wanting to look for the black window. He stared at the big trash bin behind the toy store. His feet seemed to have a mind of their own as he moved down the alley. After what happened before, Susan couldn't believe he was going back to the trash bin. But then she saw the vacant look in his eyes and heard a horn sound from somewhere. She looked around to find out where the sound came from but saw nothing. By the time she focused her attention on John, he was behind the toy store.

John's heart jumped when he saw the shiny dark window leaning against the side of the trash bin. He reached out slowly. He tapped the darkness with his finger as if bidding it to open. In an instant, the unspoken wish was granted and the window was alive with moving blurred images.

John opened his mouth in surprise. He tried to step backward, but his feet seemed stuck. He forgot about his feet, however, when the window began to focus on the depths of the world it contained. Through the window, he saw it—a huge mountain of glimmering, shiny new toys. Toys, toys and more toys were everywhere. Trains and dolls and balls and bats and cars and airplanes and a zillion other things that were made for fun were all piled on top of each other. John stared, as if in a trance.

Behind the mountain of toys, a dim blue light glowed on the horizon. John licked his lips in wonder and fascination at such treasure just beyond his grasp. And suddenly, over the top of this huge mountain of toys came a boy. The boy jumped down in leaping bounds and flying steps until he bounced right up to the edge of the window. John was looking at a dark reflection of himself. The boy on the other side of the window smiled.

"It's here. It's all here," the John on the other side of the window whispered. "Come back to us. It's your reward. You deserve it. Treasure galore. Come get it and I'll show you how."

The boy then turned and ran away. A surge of excitement filled John. This seemed to be the same place he had gone when he had disappeared. But then John noticed the long chain trailing behind the wishful boy who was bounding back up the mountain of toys inside the window. The boy disappeared over the top of the toy mountain and the long dark chain stretched tighter and tighter. That's when John felt pulled forward. He jerked back, struggling to keep his balance, but the dark chain came right out of the window and was stretched tight around his neck as if it had been there all along.

Susan watched the scene with stunned disbelief. Though she couldn't see the chain, she knew something was wrong. She began moving toward John on her bike, but it was too late. John struggled. But the harder he pulled, the more he felt pulled back, as if he were pulling himself. "John, wait!" Susan yelled. John turned his head to see Susan, but the power of the chain was too much. John reached out to brace himself against the dark window. But the instant his hand touched the darkness this time, he was sucked through into the world beyond the window.

"John!" Susan screamed. She skidded to a halt in front of the dark window.

Just beyond the surface she saw two Johns. One seemed to be struggling with the other. A distant barren hill loomed in the background in front of an eerie blue light.

"John, John, come back," Susan called. The two boys faded into the darkness as the window went blank. Susan felt a fear welling up inside of her. She gripped the handlebars of her Spirit Flyer tighter. She stared at the black window and leaned closer. She knew better than to touch it.

Just then her own reflection came into focus out of the shiny darkness. Only this wasn't a true reflection, but a picture of Susan. The Susan in the window wasn't on a bike.

"If you don't want to play, go away," the Susan inside the window sneered. "I've got your number. I'll get you soon enough."

Susan screamed as she rolled backward on her bicycle. The reflection in the window began to laugh.

Just then a horn blew, snapping the hold of fear that had gripped the girl. She cocked her head and looked both ways up and down the alley, trying to see where the sound had come from. That's when she saw Barry Smedlowe step from behind a small wooden shack just thirty feet away.

"I saw the whole thing," Barry said in a nervous, shaking voice. Then he frowned, staring at the black window. "I want to know where your brother went and what kind of game you Kramars are playing. What are you hiding? Tell me right now or I'll blast you."

Barry pulled out a slingshot from behind his back. Susan turned her bicycle to face him.

"I'm not sure what's going on," Susan said truthfully, staring at the slingshot. She was so confused and bewildered at the moment, she hardly felt afraid of Barry's threat.

As he loaded a rock, the old red Spirit Flyer suddenly leaped toward Barry. The pedals began turning by themselves as the bike quickly picked up speed. Susan lost her balance for an instant. Instinctively she leaned forward to get a better grip on the handlebars.

Barry yelped when he saw Susan charging straight at him. He dropped the slingshot and rock and started running down the alley. But the Spirit Flyer was gaining speed. The big balloon tires ate up the pavement behind the boy's fleeing steps. Barry looked over his shoulder and his eyes went wide with fear as the big red bike brushed against his heels.

"Look out, you crazy . . ."

Barry yelled and dove for the pavement as the old red bicycle lifted up into the air. The big tires of the Spirit Flyer zoomed over the boy's head, missing him by inches. Barry thought Susan had somehow jumped the bike, but when he looked up, he was amazed to see the old red bicycle climbing higher into the air. The bike was as high as the roof of the hardware store and going higher, when all of a sudden there was a humming sound. Then right before his eyes, the Spirit Flyer disappeared into thin air.

A MOUNTAIN OF TOYS

7

Susan barely had time to catch her breath before she popped back into the normal sky. Everything was fluffy white below her feet. The humming noise had stopped. The wheels of the old red bicycle were just skimming above the tops of the clouds. The fear Susan had felt in the alley had changed to excitement as the bike glided silently through the crisp air. Things had happened so quickly that she didn't realize where she was until the old red bike dove down through the misty clouds.

When she broke through, she was high above the Centerville dump. The mounds of garbage looked small and tiny. And then she saw John. He was sitting on the ground in the freshly dug pit the two children had been in the day before.

The Spirit Flyer glided quickly down toward the dump. Susan held on, letting the old red bicycle go where it willed. As she flew over the mounds of garbage, the awful smells drifted upward.

The bike carried her over to the large pit and came to a gentle halt by John. But instead of landing, the bicycle hovered in the air, the big balloon tires three inches above the ground. Since the bicycle hadn't landed, Susan figured she shouldn't get off.

John was still sitting down. He looked at Susan, then looked down at his open hands which were filled with the fine gray powder of crumbled ashes. He slapped his hands together and the sooty powder filled the air. His face seemed disturbed as he stared at the black clouds around him.

"They were all right here," John mumbled. "I had them."

"What happened?" Susan asked. As soon as she spoke she remembered her resolve that she wasn't going to speak to John. But since the words were already out of her mouth, Susan felt some of her anger melt away. She also figured that since the Spirit Flyer had carried her to John, it didn't make any sense not to talk to him. Besides, he looked so confused she felt sorry for him.

The boy grabbed the old red bicycle to steady himself as he struggled to his feet. "I went through that black window again," John said.

"I tried to stop you," Susan said, "but I was too late."

After a moment of silence they heard a sound in the distance. "Sounds like a truck is coming," John said. "We better hide."

John began sprinting for the far end of the pit. Susan turned the bike in midair and pedaled after him. John darted behind a pile of garbage and peeked out toward the entrance of the dump. Susan glided up behind him.

She put her foot on the brake and the old red bicycle slowly dropped down until both wheels rested on the garbage-covered ground. "Why are we hiding?" Susan asked.

"Shhhh!" John said. He pointed toward the entrance to the dump. A big tractor-trailer truck pulled in. With a hiss of brakes and a grinding of gears, the big truck backed up to the freshly dug pit

While the motor ran, two men in gray uniforms got out and walked to the back of the truck. The men opened the big doors. One man pulled down the ramp while the other man jumped inside. He loaded a box on the handcart and rolled it down the ramp. He dumped the box on the dirt almost exactly where John had been sitting, then pulled the cart back up the ramp. The other man had loaded up a box by then and did the same as the first man.

"That's the truck that was at the toy store," John whispered.

"But why are they here?" Susan asked. "Phew! It really stinks in this place."

"Maybe they have some trash to dump before they deliver those old toys," John said.

The two children watched quietly as the men unloaded box after box. The ground was soon covered with the boxes.

"That's a lot of trash," John said as yet another box came down the ramp.

Susan frowned as she watched. "I think they're dumping the whole load," she said.

"But they have toys in there. Why would she dump out good toys?" John asked.

The men worked even faster. One of them pulled up the ramp and they began just throwing the boxes off the back of the trailer. Within minutes the whole truck was empty and a small mountain of boxes lay in the pit. The last box hit with a crunch and burst open part way. Something in bright colors spilled out, but it fell behind the other boxes before John or Susan could see what it was.

Then the men rolled a black ten-speed bicycle to the rear of the truck. With one big push, it sailed out and crashed on top of the boxes.

"I told you," Susan said. "She's throwing away all the toys."

"It must be trash," John said. "But that bicycle looks new to me."

The two men closed the big doors on the back of the trailer. They were talking, but the two children couldn't hear what they were saying.

The men walked to the front of the truck and got inside, slamming the doors shut. Then the truck moved forward slowly, heading out to the old dump road.

When the sounds of the truck died away, John stood up straight. "I'm going down there."

"Did you hear a horn?" Susan asked, cocking her head.

"No," John said, stopping to listen. "Let's go down there and open those boxes right . . ."

"I heard it again. It sounds like that one I heard the other day behind the toy store, and twice this morning. But who would be blowing a horn out here?"

"Maybe it's a car on Crofts Road or someone on a farm around here."

"It doesn't sound like that," Susan said, turning her head. "It's almost like it's inside my head."

"Great," John replied. "You can stay and listen to horns in your head. I'm going exploring."

John picked his way over the trash until he got to level ground.

"I don't think you should," Susan called after him. But it was too late. John was already running toward the pit of freshly dumped boxes.

High up above, Nail the crow which had been circling in the air swooped down like a bullet when it saw the boy running toward the pit. The crow settled on an old black tire and watched as the boy picked his way through boxes. Mrs. Happy had given the bird strict instructions to keep an eye on both children, especially Susan.

"John, come back!" Susan called.

The boy stopped and turned. He waved to his cousin.

"Come on," John yelled. "It's ok. No one's here."

Susan pushed her Spirit Flyer out into the open. She began to pedal and aimed the old red bicycle for the sky. When both tires were three feet off the ground, she skimmed over the heaps of garbage and junk.

John had just reached the bare dirt pit when Susan braked beside him.

She took her foot off the brake and the old red bike hung in the air, two feet off the ground.

"Come help me look," John said. He ran over and pulled the black bicycle away from the boxes. The bike was a Goliath Cobra Deluxe. The thin tires were tight and full of air. "This bike is like new!"

"I have a bad feeling about this just like I do about Mrs. Happy," Susan said. She watched John set the bike carefully on the ground. The bike did appear to be in excellent condition.

"I just can't believe it," John said, staring at the bike.

"I think we should leave. It smells terrible out here, like somebody dumped a dead animal or something. This whole place is creepy."

"What's a little stink when treasure is to be found?" John said with glee. He ran to the first cardboard box and kicked it.

He yelled when the box barely budged. He hopped on one foot, holding his other foot with both hands.

"That felt like bricks," John said. He tried walking on his sore foot and limped around in a circle.

"Let's just leave. The smell is making my head hurt."

"Leave then," John said. "Or go wait over by the gate. I aim to find out what's in these boxes."

John limped over to the box that he had kicked. "It's taped shut. But never fear. I have my pocket knife."

He flipped open the short blade and slit the tape on the box. When he pulled open the flaps, he paused.

"I don't believe it," he said. "It's baseball gloves. It's full of 'em. I cut the leather on the thumb of this catcher's mitt, but the rest are all ok." He pulled the flap back so Susan could see. John ran to the next box. He slit the tape so fast, he nicked his finger. "Look," he cried with greed. "Dolls and junk. It's all new, new, new. I don't believe it." This must be it. These are my toys. I knew they would be here!"

"There's something wrong about this, John," Susan said. Just then she heard the sound of the blowing horn again. She listened carefully, then looked at her Spirit Flyer.

"Go away then, if you're scared," John said nastily. "But I'm the rich one. I get all the loot. Finders keepers."

"That's it!" Susan said. "That's why the horn was blowing. The horn is warning me!"

Just then a rumble filled the air. Neither child had noticed, but clouds had been gathering overhead for some time. A puff of wind swept over the dump.

"Yuck, this smell is terrible," Susan said. "I feel like I'm suffocating. I'm getting out of here." She began pedaling and turned the Spirit Flyer in the air.

"Wait!" John yelled as she pedaled away. "I'm going to need help with this stuff. At least carry a few gloves with you!" But Susan was already halfway to the front gate. John waved at her to come back. She shook her head. "Chicken!" John yelled. "It's just a little stink. I'm going to be rich! I knew it, I just knew. This is it!"

John jumped in the air with glee. But when he came down, his feet slipped on the dirt and he fell. That's when saw the shiny black surface underneath the dirt. He sat up and brushed away some dirt. Just an inch below the surface he uncovered more of the black shiny material that looked like black plastic or glass. Then he realized what it was—the black window.

John frowned. The black surface below the dirt made him feel uneasy. But as he looked out over at all the opened and unopened boxes, his fear was replaced by desire. "It feels solid enough," John said. He stomped on the ground. The black surface felt as hard as rock. Thunder rumbled in the sky. The clouds above were swirling together in dark patterns.

"I better hurry," John said. "I just can't leave all this stuff out here. But what should I pick up first?"

He ran to a closed box and slit the tape with the knife. Little plastic action figures fell onto the ground still in their packages. John smiled and ran to the next box. He yelped with delight when he saw it was model trains and track. The next box held more train stuff. The box after that was full of expensive leather footballs.

"I'm rich. I'm rich!" John shouted, running to rip open the next box. The boy was so excited he forgot everything but his sudden good fortune.

But at that moment, a loud screeching noise shook the air and earth. The pile of boxes and toys began to shake and tumble. The whole dump seemed to be in the middle of an earthquake!

John tried to run, but fell down, hitting his nose on the hard black surface. He stood up. Through the dust and shaking boxes, he could see more of the black window. It seemed enormous, as big as the pit itself.

John staggered to his feet and began running. As soon as he hit the bare dirt, the noise and shaking stopped. John paused, then turned and looked back. Several of the boxes had broken open, spilling toys out everywhere.

Susan had watched the whole thing happen with great concern. She quickly turned her Spirit Flyer around in midair and flew to John's side.

"What was that?" she asked.

But before John could speak, the boxes and toys out in the center of the pile moved again. Both their mouths dropped open when they saw the head of a boy rise up in the middle of the toys. A baseball mitt was on top of his head. He turned around slowly and looked over to the children. Even with a catcher's mitt on his head, there was no mistake; the boy looked just like John Kramar, only you could almost see through him as if he were a ghost.

"John!" Susan whispered.

The ghostly John smiled. He lifted the baseball mitt off his head and looked straight at the real John.

"We made a deal," the ghostly boy said in a quivering voice. "Do you want the toys, or don't you?"

A SPIRIT FLYER RESCUE

. . . .

8

Both children watched with open mouths as the ghostly John began sorting through the toys and boxes. One by one, he carefully picked up the toys and began putting them in a pile.

But before he had collected more than seven or eight toys, a box flipped over and then another. The ghostly John stopped and looked as the other children stared. Something was moving between the boxes, rustling and bumping as it went. A screeching, metal noise suddenly filled the air again, sounding like huge freight-train wheels grinding on gravel. More and more boxes moved and fell over. The thing that was causing the noise was slowly moving among the boxes.

Then they could see it. At first Susan thought it was a giant snake. But as it knocked more boxes out of the way, she saw that it was a huge chain moving heavily and slowly through the trash. It slid along, then disappeared back into the trash.

The ghostly John looked worried. Then John and Susan saw why. A dark metal hook the size of a garden hoe was rising up from out of the boxes. The hook's sharp point was bigger than a man's hand. It moved slowly toward the ghostly John. Before he could turn to run, the hook jerked down and seemed to catch on something. John thought he heard a clink.

The hook disappeared into the trash. The ghostly John struggled and pulled back against some invisible force. Then he fell down into the pile. He looked over at John hopelessly for an instant before going under. Then everything was quiet.

That's when Susan and John had seen enough. Susan was on her Spirit Flyer in a flash. John had picked up the Goliath Cobra Deluxe and was rolling it toward the front gate. But he had only gone two steps when he was jerked back. John fell down on the dirt and was clinging to the Goliath bike, but all the while he was being pulled back toward the pile of toys. He felt as if he was being dragged like a dog on an invisible leash. He tried to dig in his heels, but hit the shiny black surface just below the dirt. The window seemed to be everywhere.

"Susan!" John yelled.

Susan braked in midair at John's cry. When she saw him sliding backwards, she turned the old bike around.

It all happened so fast. She dove down into the pit holding onto her handlebars with one hand. Her other hand reached out for John as he let go of the black bicycle and reached up toward her. In an instant, as they locked hands, the mysterious pull was broken. John sailed easily up into the air. Susan held on and aimed the bicycle higher. John swung his leg over the back fender and held onto Susan's waist.

The Spirit Flyer was soaring high into the air toward Centerville within seconds. John looked back at the dump below. When he saw the new bicycle and the big pile of toys still waiting, his racing heart paused.

When they got close to the Sleepy Eye, Susan guided the bike down closer to the dump road. They were one foot off the ground as they passed over the old bridge that crossed over the river.

The tires of her bike touched down slowly on Crofts Road. John hopped off the back fender. Susan braked to a stop. They looked at each other without speaking, trying to catch their breath.

"I don't know when I've been that scared," Susan blurted out. "That was . . . spooky."

John nodded. He didn't say anything. In spite of everything that had happened, the instant he felt safe he began thinking about all the toys again. Toys and toys and more toys were just waiting on the open ground, ready to be picked up.

"We need to have a better plan," John said.

"A better plan for what?" Susan asked.

"To pick up the toys, of course," the boy said. "I also want to get the Goliath Cobra Deluxe. They're worth over two hundred dollars."

"Are you crazy?" Susan asked. "You mean you'd still go back out there, after all of that? I don't believe it."

"But those toys are probably worth thousands of dollars," John said.

"I'm telling Dad," Susan said. "I'm telling him and Mom everything that happened, and they won't let you go back out there. I want you to tell me what's going on!"

"Maybe Uncle Bill would want to help me get the toys," John said, ignoring Susan. "I wouldn't be as afraid with him there, would you?"

"Now I know you're crazy," Susan said. "I can't believe you're seriously even thinking about those stupid toys."

"Maybe we should tell Mrs. Happy that those men didn't deliver those toys like they said they were supposed to," John said. "Maybe she would offer us a reward for telling her what really happened."

"I don't trust her," Susan said. "I have a bad feeling about this whole thing, and it just keeps getting worse."

"You and your feelings," John said. "You have to go by facts. That's what Uncle Bill always says."

"She seems suspicious to me," Susan said. "That black window was behind a store that she just bought. Besides, you were the one who was so suspicious yesterday. You wanted to go there in the first place because you thought there might be something wrong at the toy store."

"I've changed my mind," John said. "She's just a nice old lady."

"I don't think so. But maybe we *should* pay her a visit," Susan said. "I'd like to ask this Mrs. Happy a few questions. Maybe we should take Dad along too."

"And make her mad?" John asked. "The Grand Opening Celebration is this Friday. If you go accusing her of stuff like you did before, we won't even get a broken checker."

"I didn't accuse her of anything, and I won't," Susan said. She was beginning to get angry with John again. She felt as if she had practically saved his life, and he hadn't thanked her. He hadn't even apologized for lying the day before. And not only that, they were arguing with each other over a bunch of toys.

"If we do go, I say play it smart and just mention that her toys seemed to have been mistakenly dumped," John said. "Let's just ride by there."

"Ok," Susan said with a sigh. "I'm all for that."

She could see that John was determined to get something for all his troubles, though she felt that all they were going to get was more trouble. John hopped back on the rear fender of the Spirit Flyer. Neither one spoke as they rode.

When they turned the corner on Main Street, they stopped. A big tractor-trailer truck was parked in front of the toy store. Two men were unloading boxes and rolling them through the door. Mrs. Happy was on the sidewalk. Nail was sitting on her shoulder.

"That was quick," John said. "She's getting new toys already. Let's go see."

At that moment Susan heard a horn blow. She felt sure the sound was coming from the horn on her Spirit Flyer. The sound stopped.

"I heard the horn again," Susan said. "I think the Spirit Flyer is trying to warn us of danger."

"Sure, Susan," John said. He laughed at her and began walking toward the toy store.

Susan pedaled slowly down the block. They passed the truck and watched the men quietly. Tall words were written on the side of the trailer: "Goliath Toys—Giants of Fun, Fun, Fun!!!"

Susan pedaled over to the store. When the old woman turned and looked at them, Susan felt uneasy again.

"Hi, Mrs. Happy," John said. The old woman smiled warmly at John. Then she stared at Susan. The crow on the old woman's shoulder leaned forward to look more closely at Susan. "Mrs. Happy, as a good citizen, I think I really should tell you about something strange that just. . ."

"I'm very busy right now, young man," Mrs. Happy said. "I have this whole load of toys to check. They've just been processed and returned. I would love to stop and chat with you children, but I just can't. Please come by for our Big Grand Opening Celebration and get some free toys. They're new and improved, you know, besides being extra superspecial."

"But that truck threw out a whole load of your toys at the dump a little while ago," John said.

"I really can't stop to talk. I'm sorry," Mrs. Happy said. The twinkle disappeared from her eye as she looked down at John.

"Can't stop, can't stop," Nail the crow said in a squeaky voice.

"Let's go," Susan said.

"Bye," John said. But the old woman didn't seem to hear. Nail the crow, however, kept looking at John and Susan. The dark little bird watched the children pedal away. When they turned the corner, the crow fluttered up into the sky.

Barry Smedlowe stepped out of the toy store onto the sidewalk and watched Nail fly away. He struck his fist into the palm of his hand.

After John, Susan and the strange black window had all disappeared in the alley behind the toy store, the leader of the Cobra Club had been both afraid and frustrated by the whole incident. Barry had ridden his bicycle around town looking for the two Kramars like a hungry shark searching for escaped prey. He had stopped by the toy store when the Goliath Toy truck arrived. Mrs. Happy had let him come inside to watch the men unload the boxes. When Susan and John rode past the store, Barry had hidden behind a large box by the front door. He was sure that neither of the Kramar children had seen him.

"What was John Kramar saying about a load of toys at the dump?" Barry asked as Mrs. Happy carried a small box from the truck into the store.

"I'm rather busy now," the old woman said over her shoulder. "Perhaps it's time you ran along."

"But John said he saw a bunch of your toys that someone threw out at the . . ."

Mrs. Happy closed the front door. Barry looked up and down Main Street. In a moment he was running for his bike which was locked in the clubhouse behind the alley. Mrs. Happy pulled back one of the dark curtains and watched the boy running down the street. A smile spread across her face.

"The little fools are as predictable as a clock," she said to herself. Then she began to laugh. "Too bad that birdbrain isn't here to see an operation executed in the proper fashion. I'll deal with him when he returns."

She walked back to her desk and sat down in front of the black window. She got a long hook from her carpetbag. She watched the president of the Cobra Club pedaling down Crofts Road. She smiled once more, then leaned back in her chair, the hook waiting in her hand. At the right moment, she pushed the hook through the darkness and pulled hard

THE TOY CAMPAIGN

9

Barry Smedlowe turned onto the old dump road at breakneck speed. As he guided his black ten-speed between the deep potholes and ruts, he tried to imagine what kind of treasures awaited discovery at the dump. Since he had heard John Kramar talking about toys at the dump before, he was sure there must be something to the story

He was panting heavily by the time he passed through the old iron gate. The dump seemed abandoned. The mounds of trash were quiet under the darkening, cloudy sky. The smell of rotten garbage was so bad that it made his eyes water.

Then he saw the freshly dug pit and the pile of boxes and forgot about the awful odors. In front of the pit, he saw a bicycle lying in the dirt. Though it might have just been his watery eyes, the large pile of boxes glimmered like a mirage in the desert. Barry's heart pounded as he pedaled closer for a better look.

Barry stopped and inspected the abandoned Goliath Cobra Deluxe. He looked around the dump, wondering who could have left the bicycle. Then he saw an opened box that appeared to be full of brand-new baseball gloves.

"Someone did dump a load of toys," Barry whispered to himself in awe. He rolled toward the small mountain of boxes and trash. He was about to jump off his bike when he noticed the black shiny surface half hidden under the dust.

Barry stopped the front wheel of the bike at the edge of the black surface. He leaned over the handlebars and looked down. He wasn't exactly surprised to see his dark reflection looking back at him. But the black glass or plastic or whatever it was seemed vaguely familiar.

"I wonder if it's some kind of glass," Barry said to himself. He rode out over the black surface, staring at the box full of baseball mitts. But before he got five feet, the bike stopped moving. Barry looked down and was surprised to see both tires of the Goliath Cobra Deluxe rapidly sinking down into the black surface as if it were a pit of tar.

Barry yelled just as the black surface gave way completely. In a instant, both bike and boy were swallowed up. Then everything was darkness.

Barry was still yelling when he heard the sound of a pop! He blinked his eyes and shook his head.

"Nice of you to drop up, my boy," Mrs. Happy said, putting a long black hook away into her carpetbag. The other hook faded in her hand before Barry could see what was happening.

Barry shook his head and stared at the smiling old woman.

"Drop up?" he asked. He looked at his feet. He was still on his bike, and the bike was on top of a long black rectangle object that resembled a window. The boy dived off the black bicycle as if to get away. His Goliath Cobra Deluxe crashed to the floor.

"Up, down, sideways, it makes no difference to me," the old woman said. "You're here. And you're welcome, you lucky boy."

"Lucky?" Barry asked. "What happened? What happened to the dump?"

"You stumbled into something very big, my boy, when you stumbled into that pit at the dump," Mrs. Happy said with a smile. "Of course you couldn't quite help it. That dump is one of our testing grounds."

"Testing grounds?" Barry asked. "What are you talking about? And where am I?"

Barry looked around and saw that he was in the toy store. A workman rolled in a sealed cardboard box. The big boxes were all over the store.

"Excuse me a minute, my boy," Mrs. Happy said. "I have some work to attend to first with these men. And then I'll explain what has happened. In the meantime, have some candy."

Mrs. Happy gave Barry a purple bowl full of wrapped candies. Barry smiled when he saw them. "Sweet Temptations," he said, grabbing a handful. He quickly unwrapped two of the marble-shaped candies that looked like a cat's green eyes. "I haven't had any of these in awhile."

While Mrs. Happy talked to the men, Barry crunched up the first two candies and stuffed two more into his mouth. Bits of candy and drool dribbled down his chin. The big boy wiped it off with his sleeve and unwrapped another piece.

The workmen rolled their carts out the front door and closed it behind them. Mrs. Happy walked over to Barry.

"I've got boxes and boxes of this candy," Mrs. Happy said with a twinkle in her eye. "And I give it to all my friends. And I'm sure you'll be one of my best friends. Now tell me again. What did you say happened?"

"Well, it all started yesterday when I heard these two jerky kids, John and Susan Kramar, out talking behind your store," Barry began. Mrs. Happy nodded wearily as she listened to his story, rather bored to hear such a limited report of what she already knew. Yet she let Barry talk since she knew it made him feel important. She unwrapped another piece of candy and fed it to the boy.

"But before I could reach the pile of toys, I got sucked into that thing and ended up here. You told me you would explain what's going on," the president of the Cobra Club demanded.

"You stumbled into something very big out at the dump, my boy," the woman replied. "Very big. So big, I'm not sure I can tell you."

"Not tell me!" Barry exclaimed.

"Not unless you swear you'll never breathe a word of this secret," the old woman said. "Your very life could be at stake. In fact, the lives of every person in this town may hang in the balance of keeping this secret."

"Wow!" Barry said. "I didn't know it was that serious."

"It's more than serious, my boy," the old woman said. "But I think I can trust you. I warn you, however, if I let you in on this secret and you break the trust, you will be in more trouble than you ever knew."

"I won't tell," Barry said. "I promise."

"Good, then you won't mind signing this oath," the old woman said. She pulled out a piece of paper from nowhere, it seemed. Then she grabbed Barry's hand. She reached into her pocket with her other hand and held out a long silver needle. The sharp point glistened. "All we need is a drop of your blood on this document."

"My blood?" Barry asked, drawing back his hand. "With that thing?"

"Don't be such a baby," Mrs. Happy laughed. "You want to know the secrets, don't you? If you sign this oath, you will know things that no one knows. Good things and bad things. Things not even your parents know."

"My parents don't know much anyway," Barry said, looking nervously at the needle.

"Quit stalling," Mrs. Happy snapped. "You signed an oath just like this for the Cobra Club, did you not?"

"Well, that was a loyalty oath," the big boy said.

"So is this," the old woman replied. "And it won't hurt a bit. Do you want to know some of the most secret secrets or not?"

"I guess so . . ." Barry said.

The old woman jabbed the needle into the tip of his right index finger without hesitating. "Ooooouuuuch!" Barry yelped. He stared at the drop of blood. Mrs. Happy wiped her mouth as she too stared at the blood. Her eyes looked wild for a moment. "Well," Barry asked. "Are you going to let me sign, or am I going to sit here and bleed to death?"

"Quit complaining," the old woman said. She pressed the finger down on the piece of paper, leaving a red fingerprint.

"I don't need to sign my name?"

"A fingerprint is enough for us."

"What does that writing say?"

"It just says you've sworn to keep government secrets."

"But what do all those little words at the bottom say?"

"Just a few details and rules. We don't have time for that now," the old woman replied. She looked at the fingerprint closely. "Good. The blood has dried and the oath is complete. You are now one of us."

"Who are we?" Barry asked. "Did you say the government?"

"That's right," Mrs. Happy said. "I represent the government, or rather the government behind the government, so to speak."

"You mean like the secret service or something?" Barry asked, very impressed.

"Exactly," Mrs. Happy said. "And our company, Goliath Industries, with its smaller companies, like Goliath Toys, is working in cooperation with the government. All Goliath employees are sworn to secrecy."

"Wow!" Barry whispered. He rubbed his finger and ate another piece of candy. "But why all the secrets?"

"Because my government, *our* government, is facing an enemy invasion that could destroy all the work we've done for hundreds of years," the old woman said. "This very world is threatened, in fact. It will take some time for you to learn all the details, but I can give you the big picture, my boy, at least for right now."

"Wow!" Barry whispered again. "But what does that have to do with that thing I fell in?"

"You didn't fall, exactly," Mrs. Happy said. "You were recruited, my boy. The Bureau has been watching you for a long time. Years, in fact. You have leadership qualities. You've proven that in the time you've been president of the Cobra Club. We like your style."

"Well, I always thought I did have class," Barry said. He opened two pieces of Sweet Temptations. He popped one into his mouth and gave the other one to Mrs. Happy. "Tell me more."

"The enemy has targeted Centerville for a secret invasion," Mrs. Happy said. "Goliath Industries has plans to reopen the old factory on the outside of town soon, perhaps by the end of the summer. The factory will be used for some secret government defense projects among other things. But these plans are being threatened. Though headquarters really isn't worried, the government has seen that it needs to take more extreme measures to counter this attack to limit the spread of the enemy."

"Really?" Barry whispered. "But who's the enemy?"

"That's part of the problem," Mrs. Happy said. "Everyone is a suspect. But we do know who some of them are. You do too. In fact, you were following them today."

"You mean John and Susan Kramar?" Barry asked. "I knew they were jerks, but I didn't know they were doing stuff like that."

"Oh, they're part of the attack all right," Mrs. Happy said seriously. "We know because of the bicycles."

"You mean those junky old Spirit Flyers?" Barry asked. "But those are . . . hey, those are very peculiar bicycles."

"You yourself have witnessed some of the secret powers the enemy is practicing with those bicycles," Mrs. Happy said.

"A lot of strange things have been going on ever since John Kramar found that junk-heap bicycle at the dump," Barry said and nodded. "But I didn't know it was part of some enemy invasion."

"They're tricky, no doubt about it," Mrs. Happy said. "And powerful. The enemy has planted those bicycles in Centerville, using them for their own tests, no doubt. The Kramar children may not even be aware of what they have gotten themselves into. Then again, they may be cooperating with the enemy. In either case, we in the government have a few tricks up our sleeves also. We know that you have to fight fire with fire. That pit you stumbled into today, bringing you here, is just one of our own deeper devices. The government plans to use a number of experiments to fight the Spirit Flyer invasion. I'll let you in on a big secret. The toys we have coming in for our Big Grand Opening Celebration are not ordinary toys. We must arm this town, but in a way that won't cause alarm. We don't want people to panic."

"I can see that," Barry said, nodding his head up and down.

"But we need a person, a child on the inside, so to speak, to look out for things for us," the old woman said. "A Toy Master. And Goliath Toys thinks you're the one. The big Number One."

"Really?" Barry asked. "But why don't you do it yourself? I mean, why doesn't the government just come in here and stop the enemy?"

"It's not that simple," the old woman said impatiently. "We have rules and regulations and procedures we have to follow. We have to use human free . . . I mean, well, it's rather hard to explain. It's like that oath you signed. We needed your permission. And once you give your permission in a little small thing like that, then you are free to be used for really big important tasks. It's rather like an army fighting in a war. We in Goliath Industries are the generals and the officers, but we need able soldiers, ordinary citizens like yourself, at the front lines where the action is really taking place. So you see, you are on the front lines here in Centerville. We'll be putting a good deal of trust in you."

"Wow!" Barry whispered, feeling the pride swell inside though he wasn't really sure he understood the old woman.

"I told you we've been watching you," Mrs. Happy said. "And on Independence Day, with our Grand Opening Celebration, we'll begin our campaign to take back the lost ground the enemy has gained. First we arm them during the day, then we will enlist them all at night—when the fireworks begin. And no one can stop us."

"But what exactly are you talking about?" Barry asked. "What can those old bicycles do?"

"In the long run, make slaves of every person in this town, in this whole world, in fact," Mrs. Happy said. "Of course, that will never happen because the government is on the job. But the traitors have learned some secrets, deeper secrets, stolen secrets. That's what gives those bicycles the power they possess. We must neutralize that power."

"I've never seen bicycles like Spirit Flyers," Barry said. "They're ugly and all, but most kids would want one if they knew how they worked."

"That's the enemy's trick," Mrs. Happy said, shaking her head sadly. "Those bicycles look innocent enough, but they must be stopped. Sometimes we find it necessary to take more extreme measures to defeat them, like introducing a better line of toys. When most children see the toys we offer, they forget about ever wanting a Spirit Flyer. Toy campaigns have proven very successful in most places. The Toy Campaign here in Centerville will neutralize the enemy as we distribute our own safe products. I expect to get a lot of permission slips signed by the end of the target date. We'll have a whole town full of children ready to fight the Spirit Flyer invasion."

"But why would they forget Spirit Flyers when they can do such amazing things?" Barry asked.

"Because Spirit Flyers are just cheap imitations built on stolen se-crets," the old woman said bitterly. "These new improved toys will have deeper powers to please their owners. Centerville, like many other places, has qualified to receive these toys. For instance, we have bicycles, Goliath Super Wings, that will make the Spirit Flyers look like mere trash-heap bikes. Goliath Super Wings are so powerful next to a Spirit Flyer that it's like comparing a jet plane to a mere kite."

"Wow!" Barry said. "If I had a bicycle like that, I could be president of two or three Cobra Clubs."

"With a powerful bicycle like that, you could be the prince of this town, my boy, and probably two or three other towns."

"I could blast those Kramars right out of the sky!" Barry said. He was so excited his piece of candy popped right out of his mouth. Barry picked it up off the floor and starting sucking on it again.

"Not so fast, young prince," Mrs. Happy said. "In the right time, if you are worthy, perhaps you'll qualify. As I said, these are special toys. We will have to release the powers gradually, and secretly. Not only you, but the other children of this town must prove worthy of the government's trust. It may take some time before the total plan can be carried out."

"Well, you can count on my support," Barry said angrily. "And to think that those Kramars go around acting like goody-two-shoes citizens. I didn't realize how deep this invasion went."

"Very deep, my boy," Mrs. Happy said. "I can tell you more, but let's go back to my office. I can't say how happy I am to know that you're on the Goliath team. Remember, the key word is *secrecy*."

Barry followed the old woman to the back of the store. She picked up her basket of yarn and sat down. As she began to hook the black yarn, she told her tale, stitch by stitch, link by link and lie by lie. And Barry was hooked on her every word.

AN
UNEXPECTED
TRIP
· · · · · · · ·

10

Susan was ready to chew on her hedge trimmer by the time she and John finished mowing their last lawn of the day. Besides the threat of rain and the lost time with the morning's adventure at the dump, John had been acting like a boy lost in a day-dream. He had tried to mow too fast and left all kinds of patches and spots that had to be re-cut. Plus he had taken overly long water breaks. Susan had to go looking for him several times. She had usually found him under a shade tree holding an empty glass and looking off in the distance.

By quitting time, Susan had had it. Even though they had caught up on their day's work, Susan decided she would keep three-quarters of the money they were paid, instead of just half. In fact, when she did pocket more than her share of the money, John didn't seem to notice the loss. He pulled the lawn mower mechanically down the street still lost in his thoughts.

"Will you snap out of it?" Susan demanded.

"What's wrong now?" John asked.

"You've been acting like a sleepwalker all afternoon," Susan said.

"I've got a lot on my mind," John said. "I've been thinking of a way we can get that bike and those toys from the dump. It will be a fairly big operation. We really need a truck to do the job right, but a large car would work. Plus we're going to need a place to put them too. There's some room in the shed, but not enough for that many toys. I could trust Roger to put some in his room if I cut him in on a percentage basis, but he might want too much of a . . ."

"I should have known," Susan said. "Those stupid toys. Daddy's not going to let you anywhere near the dump when you tell him what happened this time. And you are going to tell the truth, aren't you? If you don't, so help me I'll . . ."

"I said I would," John said and sighed wearily.

"You better," Susan replied. "He probably thinks I'm crazy after that stunt you pulled yesterday. Even though you'll get in trouble, which you *should,* it will be less than if you waited. Besides, I'm getting worried about this whole business. You said that pile of toys had something to do with the time you disappeared. What's the connection?"

"I'll tell you soon enough," John said slowly. "After supper tonight, maybe. But not if you don't stop bugging me."

"You're lucky I'm even speaking to you after the way you lied yesterday," Susan said. She glared at John, but he wasn't paying attention. Susan was ready to slug him in the shoulder to get him to respond. Nothing was more frustrating than trying to argue with someone who didn't even seem to listen.

"I'm real lucky," John murmured in a monotone voice. Susan sighed out loud to show how she felt but got no reaction. At least he had agreed to come clean and tell her father about the black windows at the toy store and dump, and all the other things that had happened the last two days. But since John agreed to tell the truth so easily, Susan began to wonder if he was just putting her off. Trust could be as fragile as an eggshell, her father once told her. If it was broken by even one lie, it was difficult to repair and trust again. Susan wasn't really sure if John would do as he had promised. Since he had been in so many yo-yo crazy moods the past few weeks, nothing about his behavior would surprise her.

As they pulled the mower and other equipment up the driveway to their house, she stopped and stood in front of John.

"Remember, John," she said. "No tricks. Dad's already home and I want you to tell him before supper, ok?"

"I will," John said, a sinking feeling growing in his stomach. He suddenly felt worse than he could ever remember. This was even worse than the time he had carelessly broken his bedroom window with a baseball bat and hadn't told anyone for three days.

Deep inside, John knew there would be relief in telling the truth. Yet the boy had another reason for coming clean, more out of greed than shame. He knew that if he was ever to get all the toys at the dump and keep them, he would have to tell his uncle and aunt the whole story. Therefore, the boy reasoned that the truth would be more practical, if not less painful, in the long run.

After they put the mower and other tools away, Susan stood by the door and waited. John was carefully wiping the hand clippers with a rag. His sudden concern for orderliness didn't fool Susan a bit.

"You've got to tell them," she said, watching him carefully. "No use in stalling now."

"I will, I will," John groaned. "You don't have to gloat about it."

"I'm not gloating," Susan said defensively. "You really have a rotten attitude. You don't even act sorry. And you haven't apologized to me yet, even after I practically saved your life this morning, not to mention the embarrassment you caused me yesterday."

Just then the door into the house opened. To John it was the door of doom.

"Aunt Bernice," Susan said in surprise. Aunt Bernice was her mother's oldest sister. She lived about two hundred miles south of Centerville in a large city. "What are you doing here? I didn't know you were coming here."

"Come in, come in," Aunt Bernice said. She was a thin woman with wire-frame glasses and a beaklike nose. She wore Mrs. Kramar's apron and was holding a broom. "Your mom and dad are just getting ready to take a little trip and want to see you before they leave."

"Leave?" Susan asked. "Where are they going?"

"Better let them explain," Aunt Bernice said. "I'm fixing supper. We'll be eating at 5:15 sharp, so you kids get cleaned up. I don't want any horseplay before supper."

Susan and John stopped in the living room. Mrs. Kramar was sitting on the couch with Lois and Katherine on either side of her. Katherine's eyes were red and wet as if she'd been crying.

"What's going on?" Susan asked.

"Your mother and I are taking a little trip," Sheriff Kramar said. "We'll be going down to stay at Bernice's house, and she'll be here to take care of you children for the next couple of days."

"But why are you leaving?" Susan asked.

"Mommy's sick," whimpered Katherine. "She going to the hospital."

"Only for some tests," Mrs. Kramar said. Her face seemed thin and pale, but her smile was reassuring. "Doctor Brimberry doesn't have the equipment he needs here, and he's suggested I go."

"But what's wrong with you?" Susan demanded, suddenly feeling a knot of fear growing in her stomach.

"Nothing serious," her father said. "Your mom hasn't been feeling well lately because . . . well, she's going to have a baby."

"A baby!" Susan said. Her surprise was complete. "You can't have another baby. Aren't you too old or something?"

Mrs. Kramar laughed. John plopped down on the couch beside Katherine. He was just as stunned by the news as Susan.

"I'm not that old," Mrs. Kramar said with a smile. "We didn't plan on this baby, but your father and I are both very excited. I've been having more severe morning sickness than I had with you children, and there are some other little complications. I may have a pinched nerve in my back. So that's why I'm going to the hospital for the tests. We'll be back by Thursday evening if all goes well."

"That's right," Mr. Kramar said. "And I want each of you to be a big help to Bernice, especially you, Susan, since you're the oldest. There's really nothing to worry about. We would have told you sooner, but Doctor Brimberry didn't make arrangements until this afternoon. We've got to go now, so give your mom a hug."

Susan was still too stunned to move. She gave her mother a quick hug, then watched her go out the door. She was still standing by the big living room window as they drove away. For a moment, she felt so overcome by the rush of so many feelings, she thought she might cry just like Katherine.

"Don't be dawdling, Susan," Aunt Bernice said. "You can't come to supper with those dirty hands. They look like you've been playing in the dirt all day."

"I've been working," Susan snapped. "Of course my hands are dirty."

"Don't be tart with me, young lady," Aunt Bernice said. "I never let my Clarence and Cecilia be tart when they lived at home and I'll not have it with you."

Susan walked down the hall to the bathroom, muttering under her breath. John was standing at the sink, a smile on his face. Susan was surprised to see him so cheerful.

"I can't believe she's going to have another baby," Susan said. "I just can't believe it. They always said they weren't going to have any more children. I'll be old enough to be this baby's grandmother."

"I'm just sorry they got Aunt Bernice to stay here," John said. "She's the most bossy person I know, except for Mr. Smedlowe at school."

"She's worse than Mr. Smedlowe, I think," Susan moaned. "She always seems to pick on me, telling me to sit up straight or part my hair differently. She's never satisfied with anything."

"Dinner!" the shrill voice of Aunt Bernice filled the house.

"At least she can cook," Susan said, drying her hands. "I still can't believe it. Another baby."

Susan felt miserable all through supper. Aunt Bernice told her to sit up straight three times. John was the only cheerful one. Susan knew he didn't care for Aunt Bernice any more than she did. It wasn't until John rushed to be excused from the table that Susan finally realized why he was in such a good mood.

"I should have known it," Susan muttered. "May I be excused?"

"You didn't eat very much," Aunt Bernice said, looking down her nose at Susan's plate. "My Cecilia always ate just as much as my Clarence when they were your age."

"I guess I'm not that hungry," Susan said. And I'm not as big as a horse like your Cecilia, she wanted to say, but didn't.

"You're excused," Aunt Bernice said. "But don't be expecting to snack all night on junk foods."

Susan left the table quickly. She ran through the house, but John was nowhere to be found. Then she went into the garage. His Spirit Flyer was still leaning against the wall, the big balloon tires squashed flat. Susan ran out to the street, but John wasn't in sight. She called his name a few times, then gave up.

Susan was sure she knew where he had gone. That's why he had been so cheerful at supper. He was planning all along to go to the dump and get the toys. Since her parents had left, John had wiggled out of telling her father and mother the truth of what had been going on.

"That little weasel!" Susan said and stomped her foot. She looked at her watch. It would still be several hours until dark.

Susan thought of getting her Spirit Flyer and going after him. But she knew it wouldn't change John's mind.

"Let him go," she said out loud. She closed the door to the shed and went back inside the house.

She sneaked past the living room where Aunt Bernice was watching a game show on television. She went to her room and closed the door. She put on her new glasses and looked over the books on her shelf. Soon she was reading a sad story in *The Book of the Kings* about the King Prince. Though she tried to concentrate on the story, her mind kept drifting to her mother. Having a baby was serious business. Susan was worried that her mother might really be sick.

Before she knew it, the sky was getting dark. Susan put her glasses and the book away. She then left her room to see if John had returned.

Her aunt was still watching television. Susan walked quietly through the house to the garage. She had been there less than a minute when John rode into the driveway on a black ten-speed bike.

John parked the bicycle in the center of the garage. He swung his leg over the seat. He looked unhappy.

"Where's all the loot?" Susan asked. "I see you brought back that bike."

"You won't believe what happened," John said. "It's terrible. I knew I should have gone back earlier today. I just knew it."

"Somebody beat you to the treasure?" Susan asked.

"Not exactly," John replied and gave a big sigh. "Roger rode me out there on his bike. I decided I needed some help. Besides, I wanted somebody to be there just in case, you know . . . something strange happened. Anyway, I told Roger all about the toys."

"Did you tell him about that boy and the hook and the big chain?" Susan asked.

"Well, not really," John said. "I didn't want to go into that. It would be hard to explain, and he'd probably think I'm crazy. Not that it matters, because he probably thinks I'm crazy anyway. We got to the dump with plenty of daylight left, but the whole area where we were is covered with trash! I can't believe it. I don't know where it came from. The Goliath Cobra Deluxe was lying off to the side. I dug a little in the trash where the toys had been, but I didn't get very far. I know Roger must think I'm the biggest liar in Centerville. He probably doesn't believe a word I said."

"Now maybe you know how it feels," Susan said smugly.

"You don't have to gloat," John said. "That's not the worst of it either. Just as we were about to leave, Barry and half of his Dead Men's Club came riding through the gate. He acted real surprised to see the new pit filled with trash too. He was a smart mouth as usual. He said that the bike belonged to him, that he had found it and left it out there. So Roger didn't know whether to believe me or not, even about the bike. Then Barry said something about toys to Doug Barns. So he must know something. The whole thing is terrible. And it's mostly your fault."

"My fault?" Susan burst out.

"That's right," John whined. "If you hadn't been so chicken this morning, we could have gone back there and cleaned up. We could have been rich!"

"But we had work to do," Susan said.

"Who cares?" John said. "I could have made a fortune selling those toys."

"I can't believe you're getting so mad at me," Susan said.

"Well, if you had lost a whole truckload of toys you'd be mad too," John said.

"But how can you lose something you never really owned in the first place?" Susan asked.

"But they were mine, all mine," John blurted out. "That was part of the deal. . . . I mean, finders keepers, since I found them."

"I think you've gone crazy over those stupid toys," Susan said.

"This is the worst thing that has ever happened to me in my life," John moaned. "The toys are buried, and Roger thinks I'm crazy. What else could go wrong?"

"Why didn't you ride your Spirit Flyer to the dump?" Susan asked.

"The tires won't pump up," John said. "The air keeps coming out from somewhere. I've tried two times. It's like that stupid bike has something against me. It figures. At least now I've got a bike that will work."

"You shouldn't call your Spirit Flyer stupid," Susan said seriously. "With an attitude like that, no wonder it won't work. You told me yourself that unless you . . ."

"Don't tell me what I said," John interrupted. "If it hadn't been for you, none of this would have happened. I just knew I should have gone right back to get those toys."

"Well, I hope you aren't planning on skipping your work tomorrow just so you can go dig in the garbage," Susan said when she saw the look in John's eye. "We've made commitments to those people."

"I'll do whatever I please," John said defiantly. "And you can't stop me."

John pushed the Goliath Cobra Deluxe past Susan and parked it against the wall. Then he walked into the house without another word. Susan went over and sat on her Spirit Flyer. She rolled outside and rocked back and forth. The clouds above were swirling in dark masses. As it got dark, a few drops of rain began to fall. Then the rain came harder. Susan went back inside the garage and closed the big door. If the rain continued through the morning, they wouldn't be able to mow lawns tomorrow, and they'd get behind in their work.

Susan sighed and went into the house. Aunt Bernice was still staring lifelessly at the television. "At least when she's watching TV, she's not picking on me," Susan mumbled to herself.

John and her sisters were in their rooms. Susan went to bed, listening to the falling rain.

She dreamed about the day's adventures, only things were mixed up. Instead of John, she was the one who had a ghost coming up out of the pile of toys. Then she saw the awful hook and the terrible chain.

That's when she woke up. The house was quiet. She got a drink of water from the kitchen and went back to bed. She wished her mother and father were home. As she drifted into sleep, she whispered all her wishes to the kings.

THE NEW IMPROVED TOY STORE

· · · · · · · ·

11

The rain lasted just long enough to wash the dust off of Centerville so everything seemed fresh and new on Wednesday morning. Susan was the first one in the kitchen for breakfast. Aunt Bernice had made oatmeal, which Susan didn't like, but ate anyway. John complained because there were no raisins in it. Aunt Bernice told him to eat and hush.

It was Susan's turn to wash the breakfast dishes and John's turn to dry. John had only dried two bowls when he got a phone call. After he hung up, he looked excited.

"Roger called and said something was happening down at the toy store," John said. "Let's go see."

"We have to finish the dishes," Susan said. "Or rather, you have to finish drying. I'm done."

She smiled and let the water drain out of the sink. Aunt Bernice came into the kitchen to inspect the children's work. Susan went to her room. She looked in the mirror for a few moments, then took her glasses off and left them on the dresser. As she passed through the kitchen, Aunt Bernice was giving John stern instructions on how to clean up. Susan smiled and went into the garage.

John dried the dishes as quickly as he could without having to do them over. Even so, Aunt Bernice made him wash all the counter tops and the table with a wet sponge. John was ready to jump out of his shoes by the time he found Susan.

"I guess we'll have to wait until it dries to cut the grass anyway," Susan said. "But we still have plenty of lawns to mow today."

"I'll help, but let's just ride by the toy store first," John said quickly. He grabbed the newly found Goliath Cobra Deluxe and hopped on. He rolled down the driveway and out into the street. As Susan got on her old red bicycle, she felt sad that John wasn't even trying to ride his Spirit Flyer.

She caught up with him at the corner. As they rode toward the toy store, Susan wondered once more about all the changes that had come into their lives in just a few short days. Yet deep down, she felt that she was seeing the pieces of a puzzle that would make sense if only they were put together in the right way. Mrs. Happy. The black window. John's disappearance. The toy giveaway. The fireworks display. The Spirit Flyers. Somehow they were all connected.

"If only I could *see it,*" the girl thought. "I wish Grandma and Grandpa Kramar had come to stay with us. He knows a lot about the Deeper World and this kind of thing."

Susan sighed. As she pedaled, she couldn't shake off the feeling that something bad was happening to her town. When she and John got to the town square, they saw children running toward Main Street. Susan pedaled faster and turned the corner.

A huge new sign over the toy store blinked on and off in purple neon letters: HAPPY TOY STORE.

"How ugly," Susan groaned out loud when she saw the flashing purple letters.

A large group of children had gathered in front of the big plate glass windows. John shot out ahead, but Susan pedaled more slowly. She rode to the opposite side of the street being careful of moving cars. From the distance she saw a huge banner stretched across the brick wall just above the big front windows:

****

NEW IMPROVED GRAND OPENING CELEBRATION!!!
INDEPENDENCE DAY JULY 4TH!!!
FREE TOYS FOR ALL!!!

****

Susan rode slowly toward the store for a better look. The black curtains were gone. Four giant pictures were in the windows. The two pictures on the left side of the door were of a sad looking boy and girl. Anyone could tell that these children were sad and bored. The words above the picture said: "Is this you? Don't be an Un-Happy girl or boy!"

The two pictures on the other side of the door were just the opposite. A girl and a boy had armfuls of toys and big knowing smiles on their faces. The words read: "This can be you!!! Be Happy at Happy Toys!!!" Loads of toys were underneath the sign, jumbled all together in bright colors. Several noses were pressed against the glass to get the closest look possible. A few children were shoving one another. A big boy stepped back and bumped into Susan, making her lose her balance.

"A person could get hurt around here," Susan muttered to herself. She walked the old red bicycle slowly out of the crowd of children and circled around, heading for the town square. More of Centerville's youngest citizens were running toward the toy store. Susan dodged them as she rode down the street.

At the corner, Barry Smedlowe shot out in front of Susan. She stepped back quickly on the brake to avoid a collision.

"Out of my way, you idiot!" he yelled as he skidded to avoid her. The leader of the Cobra Club lost control of his bike and slid into a parking meter. Both boy and bike hit the sidewalk in a clatter. Barry jumped up quickly, his face beet-red with anger. "You're trying to kill me!" he accused.

"I am not," Susan replied. "You just don't know how to ride a bicycle."

Then she laughed. That only made Barry more angry. He shook a finger at Susan.

"I've been watching you," the big boy said. "I know all about those bicycles and things you're doing. You don't fool me."

"You ought to be watching where you're going instead of snooping," Susan replied.

"You just wait," Barry threatened. "You think those junky old bikes are so special. But when I get my new bike, it will make those ugly Spirit Flyers look like . . . like kites."

Susan smiled as she rode past Barry. Though he shouted at her as she drove away, none of his threats made sense. Susan rode around the square once. Then John rode up beside her.

"Let's go check on the Blake's grass," Susan said. "Maybe it's not too wet to cut."

John nodded. They headed down Tenth Street. As they got near the sheriff's office, they saw Mrs. Happy walk out the front door. The old woman smiled warmly at the two children as they rode past her.

"What was she doing?" John asked.

"Let's find out," Susan replied. The children parked their bikes and ran up the steps.

Inside the office, George was behind the counter in his wheelchair. He smiled when he saw them.

"Did your father and mother get off ok?" George asked.

"Yes," Susan said. "You know all about it, don't you? Dad didn't tell us until the last minute."

"Well, he told me because he needed to," George said. Susan liked George, but she felt sorry for him because he was in a wheelchair. George had been in an accident a long time ago and had a permanent injury. He never said much about it though. He was a good worker, Susan knew.

"We saw Mrs. Happy leave," John said. "We wondered what she had to say."

"Yeah, what did she want?" Susan asked.

"Why all the interest?" George asked. He looked carefully at the two children.

"Since Mrs. Happy's new in town, we were just curious," Susan said.

"She was in here making arrangements for the July Fourth Celebration," George replied.

"Is that all?" John asked. "She didn't say anything about someone losing a truckload of toys, did she?"

"Nope, nothing like that," George said. He wheeled over to the desk.

"Did Mrs. Happy seem, well, strange to you?" Susan asked. "I think that Happy is an odd last name."

George leaned back in his chair. He smiled and shook his head. "Well, she may be a little eccentric," George said. "She's very wealthy, apparently. I've heard she's a distant relation to the Potter family. This is all barbershop gossip, so it may or may not be true. I believe someone said she changed her name a long time ago because it was one of those foreign names that are hard to pronounce. But it's a free country; she can call herself whatever she wants. Anyway, her family 'got fat' as she put it, on television advertising or something like that. She sure seems to know how to advertise her store. She's changed things in a hurry."

"I think she looks like Mrs. Santa Claus," John said.

"Maybe that's why she's going to give away free toys," Susan grunted.

"She seems nice enough to me," George said. "She's going to open her toy store right after the parade on July Fourth and give away the free toys then."

"Well, I'll be there for the free toys," John said.

"With every other kid in town I bet," Susan added. "The way she has the toy store fixed up now is so fancy compared to the way it was before. We'll have kids from all over the county coming here with a toy store like that. I think that purple blinking sign is ugly."

"She seems to know her business," George said. "She said she would give out numbers to all the children who want one sometime in the next couple days. That will make it less confusing for picking up a free toy. It makes a lot of sense to me. From what she's said, they will be nice gifts, too."

"I wonder what they could be?" John asked.

"You'll just have to wait until July Fourth like everyone else," George replied. "The Goliath Toy Company has also donated some real fancy fireworks for the show that night too. The way she talks, it's going to be a display of fireworks that Centerville won't forget for a long time."

"I bet it will be. It just seems like an awful lot of money to spend just to get a toy store started. We better go," Susan said. "Thanks, George."

"If you kids need anything while your Dad is gone, let me know," George said. "I'll be here or at home."

"Ok," John yelled over his shoulder. He was the first one outside. Susan shut the door.

Susan and John checked the Blake's lawn. The grass was long and still soaked from the night's rain. They hadn't ridden a block before they were starting to argue about what to do. John was ready to go prospecting at the dump, but Susan was against it.

"Well, I know one thing," John replied. "I know there are toys out at that dump just waiting for me and I plan to get them. If only we had more time to dig instead of mowing all these dumb lawns."

"Don't include me in your plans," Susan said. "I've told you I'm not digging in that trash and I mean it. And if you were smart, you'd forget about those stupid toys. After all the weird things that have happened out there, I can't believe you'd want to go back."

"You're just afraid," John said.

"I am afraid and with good reason," Susan said. "Something very confusing is happening around here and neither of us knows what it is, unless you aren't telling. But I know something has to be wrong. This toy giveaway and fireworks business bothers me. I just wish I could *see* what's wrong."

"What's wrong is letting a truckload of toys go to waste under tons of trash," John said. "That's what's wrong, if you ask me."

"It's more than those toys," Susan replied, pedaling slowly. She twisted the broken mirror on her handlebars so it would reflect backwards. Since there was only a sliver of the mirrored glass left, she didn't have much to look back with. But as she turned it so she could see, she suddenly stopped pedaling. She looked behind her, then back into the mirror. She rubbed her eyes and looked again.

John didn't notice Susan had stopped, but when he turned around, Susan was staring intently into the broken glass of the mirror.

"What's wrong now?" John asked.

"Nothing," Susan said excitedly. "I see something in this mirror."

"So what?" John said.

"But it's not what you think," Susan replied, her voice shaking. "It's not a reflection of what's behind me, it's a reflection of that pit out at the dump. I can see the black window. It's like a reflection back in time!"

"What?" John pedaled back to his cousin. "Let me see."

John bent around in front of Susan and stared into the mirror, but all he saw was a broken reflection of his shirt and his face.

"I don't see anything," John said.

"Let me look again," Susan replied. John stepped out of the way. She smiled. "It's all right there. You can't see it? I can only see bits and pieces, but it's like it's happening again, like a movie. The day we first got sucked through and came out of the hole. I see us."

"Are you sure?" John asked. "That's crazy."

He bent forward to look. He frowned. "I don't see anything," John said.

"But don't you see?" Susan said excitedly. "This is my Spirit Flyer. You probably aren't meant to see with this one. You couldn't hear my horn blowing either. Wait a minute, there's something else. We have . . . oh my . . ."

"What? What?" John demanded.

"We look the same, but I can see chains," Susan said. She squinted at the mirror. "They look real big and heavy too. And there's a hook. Just like that one we saw coming out of the pile of boxes."

"What chains?" John asked. "What hook?"

"I see a double of me even, just like I saw two of you," Susan cried excitedly. She stared deep into the old mirror. "Only now they are coming together as I get off of the black window. Now it's gone. How odd."

She looked at John, then back at the mirror. The glass was reflecting like a normal mirror once again.

"You saw chains?" John asked. He tried not to show the sudden stab of fear he felt inside. He dropped his head down and looked at his chest. Then he touched his neck as if he were a blind man feeling for something. His hands shook.

"What's wrong?" Susan asked. She stared at John. His mood had changed as suddenly as if someone had flicked a light switch.

"Nothing," John said. He let his arms drop to his sides. "Let's go mow

Mrs. Kimble's lawn. It's probably dry. All this talk of chains gives me the creeps."

John pedaled on ahead of her as fast as he could go. His sudden interest in the lawn-mowing business would have been encouraging under ordinary circumstances. But she could tell John was in one of his yo-yo moods.

Susan looked into the old mirror once more. She knew she had been shown the images of the dump for a purpose, but what? She felt as if she were still trying to fit the pieces of a puzzle together. But instead of solving the puzzle, the old mirror had just given her more pieces to fit into the picture.

John seemed to know a lot more than he was telling, and he was frightened. As Susan thought about all the strange events, she began to wonder for the first time if she really wanted her questions answered.

ON A
THRONE OF
GARBAGE
· · · · · · · · ·

12

The crowd of children gathered around the front of the toy store. They parted for Mrs. Happy when she arrived. For many children, this was their first time to see her. The new owner of the toy store smiled warmly at the children. Her business at the sheriff's office had gone well. And seeing John Kramar on the Goliath Cobra Deluxe put an extra spring in her step as she walked back to her store.

"She looks just like my grandmother," one girl in the crowd said.

The other children murmured in agreement, as if Mrs. Happy looked like their grandmother too. She unlocked the door and opened it. She stepped inside quickly, and carefully locked the door behind her.

Just then, Barry Smedlowe darted through the crowd on his bicycle.

"Out of my way!" he said to the other children. "Let the Toy Master through."

Barry knocked rapidly on the front door. He smiled when he saw Mrs. Happy walking toward him. The door opened.

"Just the boy I want to see," Mrs. Happy said with a big smile. The other children pressed around the door groaned as Barry went inside. The door shut in their faces.

"Your store really looks nice," Barry said.

"Come in, come in," Mrs. Happy said. "Since you're going to be the new secret Toy Master of this town, I'll give you the first look."

The future Toy Master looked around. Overnight, the store had changed dramatically. The place was packed with toys. You could look and look and still look some more and not begin to see all the different things for sale.

"Wow!" Barry said. "Old man Potter never had toys like this."

"It's all in advertising and display, my boy," Mrs. Happy said. "Image, image, image. Those are the key words of the day. And I mean key. You have to make the best image if you want to sell toys. No one wants dull boring toys. They want fun, fun, fun. And the Goliath Toy Company is the Giant of fun. And it's the same for people."

"What do you mean?" Barry asked.

"You have to put the best smile on your face if you want to sell yourself," the old woman said. "I have big plans for you. The government has big plans for you too. We don't want you to fail us in those plans."

"What plans?"

"All sorts of things," Mrs. Happy replied. "And the first change is a new smile."

"A new smile?" Barry asked. He frowned.

"Tut-tut, frowning will never do," the old woman said. "People like people who smile. And by the way, how often do you brush your teeth? They look like they could use a good scrubbing with a steel wool pad."

"Hey, I don't need to listen to insults," Barry snarled. "So you can just shove . . ."

"Hush, boy," Mrs. Happy said. She stared so hard into his eyes that he suddenly looked down. "Now you want to be popular, don't you? You want to be the leader, don't you? When you speak, you want the others to listen and obey, don't you?"

"Yeah, I suppose so," the big boy said.

"Then be quiet and listen to me," the old woman commanded. "The key is advertising and the smile is the first advertisement others see. Now let's practice. If you want to be Number One, here's how you do it. I'm sure you've seen the hosts of those game shows on television, haven't you? I want you to smile that game-show smile. Now let's practice . . ."

The old woman talked to Barry for over a half-hour. When he finally left Happy Toy Store, he had a new improved smile on his face and a bulging brown paper sack.

The Cobra Club was waiting outside the old wooden clubhouse. Barry didn't tell them much about his meeting with Mrs. Happy, but he did tell them about all the new toys inside. Seeing their impatient glances, Barry smiled his new improved smile. He got on his bicycle and the other boys did the same. Then he pedaled around the block. The Cobra Club rode together like a pack of dogs.

"I'm going to get first choice on the free toys, and it will probably be a new bicycle," Barry Smedlowe told his gang as they pedaled past the front of the store. They looked at the pictures of the happy boy and girl and the glistening new toys behind the windows. Their mouths watered.

"What makes you so special?" Doug Barns demanded.

"Yeah?" the other boys demanded.

"Mrs. Happy told me I had first choice," Barry replied. "But I told her about the Club, and you'll be right after me. She even gave me some great candy. Have some."

Barry pulled opened the brown paper sack. He grabbed handfuls of Sweet Temptations and passed them around. He smiled his new improved smile once again.

"Great candy," the boys said, stuffing it in. They looked at the toys for a long moment, then pedaled away as more children came by to take their places.

Barry pedaled down the street. He passed out more candy as they rode, being careful to keep his balance. Soon the boys were riding out of town on Crofts Road. Barry smiled his new smile often and kept the candy flowing. When they came to the old dump road, Barry turned and crossed the bridge over the Sleepy Eye River. The other boys followed without a single complaint.

The game plan was working as Mrs. Happy said it would. Earlier in the day, the Club had refused to go out to the dump. No one really believed that Barry had seen boxes and boxes of toys just waiting to be picked up off the ground. All they had seen was a huge pile of trash. Barry was sure the toys were there. Yet he knew he would need help to dig through the trash to the treasure inside.

During his talk with Mrs. Happy that morning, Barry had mentioned the fact that his club wouldn't help him dig for the toys. The old woman seemed sympathetic. Though she would neither confirm nor deny the existence of the toys, she did promise to help Barry. She had told him all the club needed was a little bait on the hook. Then using the mysterious black window, she had shown Barry a picture of the dump, and where to find the bait. The old woman assured Barry that a good smile and the free candy would get them to the dump. And once they found the bait, the boys would be convinced to dig for more toys.

Barry passed out more candy and then shot down the old dump road. Soon the plan would be completed. Everything was going along just like the strange old woman had said. The president of the Cobra Club smiled his new improved smile this time without even trying.

While the Cobra Club was busy at the dump, Susan and John were sitting down under a large oak tree on their lunch break. They had finished the Kimble's lawn in record time. Susan was amazed at how hard and fast John could work when he set his mind to it. All morning long she had thought about what she had seen in the mirror on her Spirit Flyer.

John stood up and stretched. Then he smiled. "Since we're a little ahead of schedule, why don't we go out to the dump?"

"I knew you had to be working hard for some reason," Susan said with disgust. She dropped her apple core into her lunch bag. "I've been thinking that maybe we should go back out to the dump too. But not to get toys. I want to try something. I want to see what will happen if I look at that big pit using the mirror. Maybe it will show me something, in a deeper way."

"I don't know about that," John said slowly.

"That's because you don't have any of the instruments on your bicycle," Susan said. "In fact, you might as well not even have a Spirit Flyer at all the way you've neglected it. It's like you've traded it in for that creepy Goliath bike."

"I tried to pump up the tires," John said, bitterly. "But the stupid thing wouldn't work."

"That's because you must not trust it, deep down," Susan said simply "Otherwise you wouldn't be mad. I've read in *The Book of the Kings* that you can work with the kings' magic or against it, which is really tragic. You haven't put on any of the instruments, like the mirror or horn or generator. And you know you should. You were told to do it. No wonder your Spirit Flyer won't work. You aren't treating it right."

"Oh, go blow your nose," John grunted. "You think you know everything from a book. I'm going to the dump. Are you coming?"

"Yes," Susan said. "But I'm not going to dig in any trash."

"Will you help me carry some toys home when I find them?" John asked.

"Maybe," Susan said. "But first you have to find them."

Barry sat in a broken rocking chair on top of a mound of trash. He held a five-foot piece of iron pipe in his hand like a staff. Down below him, the members of the Cobra Club sweated in the noonday sun as they moved piece after piece of junk from the pile. The president of the Cobra Club looked like a young prince on a throne of garbage. He felt a surge of power as he looked out over his domain, the town dump.

He stood up shakily and held the iron pipe up over his head. "I claim all valuables and toys found for the Cobra Club," he shouted in a loud voice.

"Come down and help us," Doug Barns yelled back.

"I'm coming," Barry said. He had stopped digging some time ago. The only reason the other boys were digging at all was because of a catcher's mitt they had found soon after they had gotten there. Barry had actually found the mitt. It was the bait Mrs. Happy had shown him in the black window.

Once again, the old woman had been right. The baseball mitt had done the trick. They had all worked hard for an hour. Both Doug and Alvin, also known as Nose, had cut their hands on pieces of broken glass, but not seriously. They still kept digging through the trash, clearing a path as they went.

As Barry climbed carefully down through the garbage, he saw someone far away coming down the old dump road.

"To your stations!" he shouted. In an instant, the Cobra Club scrambled up over the pile of trash, following their leader. They had already hidden two times in the last hour when people in pickup trucks had unloaded their garbage.

The boys were grateful for the interruption in the work. They waited at the top of the trash pile, just out of sight. They couldn't have been more happy when they saw Susan and John Kramar ride past the gate into the dump. Barry began whispering excitedly as the Kramar children rode straight for the pile.

John was the first one to notice that a path had been cleared into the big pile of trash. As he got closer, he saw footprints on the dirt.

"Someone's been digging here," John said. "I see all kinds of footprints."

"It's probably just Mr. Braker," Susan said. She was looking at the cracked mirror on her Spirit Flyer, trying to understand how the curious old mirror might be made to work. But before she could do anything, she heard the sound of a blowing horn.

"The horn is blowing again," she said excitedly. "We better stop and—"

"Not horns in the head again," John said. "I'm beginning to think that you may be going . . ."

But before he could finish, a shriek and a shout split the air. "Strike!" a chorus of voices yelled. John looked up just in time to see the sky filled with flying trash.

"Look out!" he cried as he ran toward Susan. A broken bottle smashed on top of the trash not two feet from where he had stood. Empty cans and other garbage rained down on the two fleeing children.

When they were sure they were out of throwing range, Susan and John stopped and turned around. Barry and the other members of the Cobra Club stood on top of the mountain of trash, laughing and hooting.

"You Kramars get out of here," Barry called out. "We've claimed this as Official Cobra Club Territory, and you're not wanted."

"This is public property," John yelled back, trying not to let the frustration in his voice show. "You can't claim anything."

"You've been warned," Barry said. "Leave or else. And when you go, leave my bicycle. I own that bike you're riding and you know it."

Barry bent down and picked up another broken bottle. He hurled it with all his might. The bottle sailed through the air and crashed on the

ground twenty feet in front of Susan and John. "Let's just go," Susan said.

"I'm not afraid of him or his stupid club," John said.

"I hear the horn again," Susan said.

"What horn?" John demanded. "You're hearing and seeing things both."

"That is it!" Susan said with a smile. "The mirror must work in a *deeper* way just like . . ." Another bottle crashed just ten feet away. The Cobra Club was yelling as they stormed down the mountain of garbage, throwing things as they charged. A rock or piece of metal bounced and hit John in the shin.

"Ouch!" he said.

"I'm leaving," Susan called. She was already on her Spirit Flyer. John picked up a rock and threw it at Barry. Then he grabbed the Goliath Cobra Deluxe and took out after Susan. Susan was waiting for him at the gate.

"There's too many," she said as John rode up beside her.

"I guess you're right," John replied. "I'd still like to get off a few shots of my own."

The Cobra Club had stopped halfway down the pile and were arming themselves. Barry held up a long piece of pipe.

"We warned you to stay out of Cobra territory," he yelled, shaking the pipe.

"Come on, somebody could get hurt," Susan told John. "You couldn't get close with them up high like that. They have too much of an advantage. And what would it prove, anyway?"

John stared back at the Cobra Club. Barry and the others were yelling for them to come back and fight. When Susan pedaled through the gate, John reluctantly followed. His ears burned as hoots and jeers followed them all the way down the old dump road.

THE WARNING HORN

. . . .

13

"Don't you see? I told you the horn was blowing to warn me!" Susan said to John. "You squeeze a normal bicycle horn to warn other people. But the horn on a Spirit Flyer works the other way around."

"Maybe," John grunted. Talk about the old bicycle instruments made him feel uneasy.

The two children were in the garage looking at the mysterious old bicycles. Supper was over and John had just finished washing the dishes.

John wasn't really convinced Susan was right about the horn and mirror. Since he had never heard or seen anything to begin with, he didn't know what to think. He looked at Susan's Spirit Flyer carefully. He touched the big rubber-bulb horn lightly with his finger. Then he grabbed the bulb and squeezed. The air squished out the bell-shaped mouth, but barely made a sound.

"See, it doesn't even work like a regular horn," Susan exclaimed excitedly.

"But how do you know it was this horn?" John demanded, still unconvinced. "I didn't hear it."

"But it's probably meant just for me since it's my Spirit Flyer," Susan said. "And I think you hear it in a different way altogether. I think it's a deeper sound because it comes from the Deeper World."

The big garage doors were open and there was still plenty of light outside. Lois and Katherine were riding their smaller Spirit Flyers up and down the street in front of the Kramar house. They were zigzagging back and forth, playing some sort of game with two other neighbor children. John rubbed his chin as he looked at the horn.

"The mirror must work in a similar way," Susan said, touching it carefully. "It reflected back to that first day we went through the black window. And it must have shown me that for a purpose."

"Yeah, for what?" John asked. "We already knew we were there. So what?"

"I don't know for sure," Susan said. "Maybe it's like what Mom says about hindsight. Sometimes you see things a lot more clearly later on after something happens, only this time we saw deeper."

"So, I still don't see," John said stubbornly.

"Well, the mirror showed us wearing those chains," Susan said. "It works in a *deeper* way. We know you can't see those chains like regular everyday chains. Grandpa told us that. I also saw that hook. I wonder why it's there. We never saw that the first time we were there, but we did see it when we saw that ghostly double of you. Don't you see?"

"I don't guess I need to see anything since you're such an expert on Spirit Flyers and the Deeper World now," John accused.

"I guess you don't want to talk about it," Susan said crisply.

"Well I was the one who first had a Spirit Flyer, wasn't I?" John said defensively. "Nobody in this family knew beans about them. I got the stolen bikes back. And I was flying and dodging lightning while you all were just locked up like a bunch of . . ."

At that point a great gust of black smoke belched out of John's mouth with a long hiss. John's eyes went wide with surprise. John tried to close his mouth, but couldn't. The ugly smoke just kept spewing out and blew straight toward Susan.

Susan began to cough as the cloud of smoke surrounded her. The smoke smelled terrible and the girl felt like she was going to suffocate. She wanted to run away, but her feet seemed as heavy as lead.

"Stop it, John," Susan wheezed. "Make it stop." John shook his head helplessly. He couldn't control it. The smoke kept hissing out of his mouth. Susan backed up until she was pressed against the wall, but the cloud of smoke followed her. Then she saw her Spirit Flyer through her watery eyes. She inched through the darkening cloud of smoke toward the old red bicycle.

Just then, Lois, Katherine and two neighbor children rode up the driveway. "Look at the smoke!" Katherine screamed in delight. "Is there a fire?"

"No, it's coming out of John's mouth," Lois said. "How odd. It's like he swallowed a smoke bomb."

"What are you two talking about?" asked the neighbor girl named Betsy.

"Yeah, I don't see any smoke," said the other neighbor girl, Michelle. "But why is your sister acting like that?"

"Yeah, she looks funny," Betsy giggled. "And so does John. He looks mad. Why is his mouth open? Is he yelling at her? I don't hear anything."

"You don't see all that smoke?" Lois asked. "Are you blind?"

"It smells terrible," Katherine said. "And it's hurting Susan. See?"

"Something's wrong," Lois said. "Stop doing that, John. You're scaring me!"

"I'm sorry!" John suddenly gasped. With those words, he was able to close his mouth, which cut off the flow of smoke. At the same time, Susan grabbed the handlebars of the Spirit Flyer with both hands. The cloud of smoke was so thick around her that she could barely see. But then the smoke began to clear. Susan heard a sound like water going down a drain. When she looked down, she saw the smoke going into the mouth of the old rubber horn on her Spirit Flyer.

"The horn is sucking up the smoke!" Katherine shrieked, clapping her hands together.

"Like a vacuum cleaner," Lois added. "Look!" The smoke disappeared rapidly into the trumpet-shaped mouth of the horn. The garage was clearing.

The two neighbor children looked puzzled. Betsy looked back and forth, trying to see what the others were staring at.

"I don't see a thing," Betsy complained. "Or hear a thing."

"You guys are just playing pretend," Michelle added. "And it doesn't seem fair to play without us."

The last bit of the evil-smelling smoke swayed and curled around like a funnel cloud of a tiny tornado as it was sucked into the horn. Then the sound stopped. All four Kramar children let out a sigh at the same time.

"It's gone," Susan said, staring at the horn. "Wow! Did you ever see anything like that?" Katherine squealed.

"I think it was awful," Lois said. "What did you do, John? Were you trying to hurt Susan?"

"I wasn't trying to," John said softly. "Or maybe I was, deep inside. I mean, I was mad at her."

"What are you all talking about?" Betsy said. "It's as if you're seeing things that aren't there. I didn't see any smoke."

"That's because you don't have a Spirit Flyer," Katherine said simply. "I bet that's it, isn't it, Susan?"

"I think you're right," Susan said. She coughed to clear her throat. "I'm not sure. It seems like the longer you're around a Spirit Flyer, the more questions you have."

"You guys are a weird family," Betsy said.

"Yeah," Michelle added.

"Come on," Lois said. "Let's play bicycle tag. Betsy's it." She screamed joyfully as she shot down the driveway and into the street. The other three girls yelled and took out after her. John and Susan watched the girls playing in the street for a few moments.

"I'm beginning to see there are a lot of things I don't know," John finally said, and sighed. Susan walked over and patted him on the arm.

"It's ok, though," Susan said. "We're learning more and more and that's good. I thought the horn was just a warning device. But look what happened to the smoke. Who knows what else it can do?"

John walked over to his Spirit Flyer. He looked at the bicycle a long time. The tires looked so flat that he wondered if they were ruined. He looked up at the box that held the old worn instruments to his bike.

"I could help you put the instruments on your bike," she offered. John nodded quietly as if agreeing. But then a frown crossed the boy's face.

"But we need to go get the toys in the dump first," John blurted out. "They belong to me."

"Can't you forget about those dumb toys just for a little while?" Susan asked.

"You just don't like the idea that I found them first," John accused. His eyes suddenly went into little angry slits. "You want them for yourself. Well, I'm going to get back what belongs to me, and you won't stop me." With those words, John strode into the house, slamming the door behind him. Susan sat down on her bicycle and sighed.

"He's like a mental case or something," the girl whispered to herself. "One minute he's happy and then he blows up like a firecracker. He acts like two people. I wish I knew what was wrong."

Susan parked her bicycle and closed the garage door. If she had looked in the mirror of her old red bicycle just once more, she would have seen the answers to some of her wishes. She thought of looking, but she heard Aunt Bernice calling her from inside the house. She closed the garage door and walked wearily inside. The last thing she wanted to do was listen to the criticisms of Aunt Bernice.

Inside the dark toy store, Mrs. Happy sat before the black window and watched John Kramar storm into the house. She smiled broadly, then she sighed. Several long thin hooks were poked through the window and left dangling. The old woman wiggled one, then sat back.

"See how it's done, you birdbrain?" the old woman asked the crow who was sitting on her shoulder. "That's the way to carry out an operation. The boy was beginning to slip away and we could have been in serious trouble the way he was looking at that box of bicycle instruments, so I just reminded him of the deal he made and his reward. As long as we can keep him confused, the target day will come and he'll be eating ashes with the rest. Though the girl is quite covered in the cloud, we can still get a hook or two in for a good strong tug."

"She'll read the book again," the crow said, looking toward the window.

"True, but she's upset and won't get much out of the reading perhaps," Mrs. Happy replied. "And maybe we can even prevent her. She's feeling rather sorry for herself and abandoned by her parents. The aunt is already a sore point. Maybe we can use her."

Mrs. Happy smiled and wiggled a hook. A few seconds later, Aunt Bernice was calling Susan. The old woman and crow watched Susan walk wearily into the house.

"We'll eat ashes on this one," the old woman said with a smile as she watched Susan and Aunt Bernice begin to argue. "It's all how you work the chain. If all goes well, we'll even get to her while she dreams . . ." She began to laugh and the crow cackled too.

NEXT TO
THE LAST
IN LINE
· · · · · · · ·

14

When Susan woke up the next morning, she wished more than anything that her parents would come home. She didn't get along with Aunt Bernice at all. No matter what Susan did, Aunt Bernice always managed to find fault. Before going to bed, Aunt Bernice had criticized Susan for not cleaning up the bathroom the proper way. Susan had gone to bed mad and slept poorly. She had woken up twice from a bad dream and it had been hard to get back to sleep. By morning she was still tired and cranky.

John acted just as moody as Susan at the breakfast table. Aunt Bernice scolded them both for being sourpusses. Susan tried to ignore her. But

John couldn't hold his tongue. He muttered something under his breath, and Aunt Bernice gave his ear a big twist. John kept his opinions to himself after that, though Susan could tell he was really angry.

John was in such a bad mood by the time they finished the breakfast dishes that she wondered if he would come along to help her mow the Fenster's yard. Susan reminded him how impatient Mr. Fenster could be. John seemed reluctant and fidgety, yet she finally convinced him to help.

Mr. Fenster was pacing on the sidewalk, pulling on his little gray beard, waiting for the two children to arrive. Susan went right to work with her clippers. Mr. Fenster walked into his house. Just then, Susan saw Roger Darrow riding up on his bicycle, and she knew it meant trouble. John had just started the mower when Roger skidded to a halt by the curb. Roger looked excited and out of breath. He jumped off his bicycle and ran over to John.

"Quick! You've got to come now," Roger said. "She's giving out numbers today. I've already got mine. And lots of other kids have gotten their numbers."

"Numbers? What are you talking about?" John asked. He cut off the mower.

"Yeah, what numbers?" Susan asked. She had stopped clipping around a light post and walked over. Grass stains covered the knees of her old blue jeans and the tips of her dirty white sneakers.

"Mrs. Happy, the new owner of the toy store, is giving out numbers," Roger said. "And the lower your number, the sooner you get in the store tomorrow for her Grand Opening Celebration."

"She's giving them out right now?" John asked.

"Yeah," Roger said. "I guess it will save time to have it done early. I'm number seventeen. There should still be plenty of good toys left. She said she's going to let kids go in the store in groups of ten, so I'll be in the second group."

Roger dug into his pocket and pulled out a shiny piece of black plastic. He gave it to John. On one side was a small number seventeen stamped in white in the upper left-hand corner. On the other side were the words in tiny letters: "Goliath Toys. Giants of Fun, Fun, Fun."

"You better hurry," Roger said. "You don't want to lose out. Every kid in town will be down there in a few minutes."

"But we've just started here," Susan said. "So John can't come."

"But she's giving out the low numbers first," John said to his cousin.

"That's right," Roger said. "You can come back. The grass won't grow that fast."

"Well, I suppose I could come right back," John said.

"John, you know how impatient Mr. Fenster is," Susan said. "You have to stay and help me."

"It'll just take a few minutes," John said.

"She's giving away some free candy too," Roger said. "I got two pockets full. It's good. Want one?"

Roger put his number away and pulled out a piece of candy and gave it to John.

"Sweet Temptations? I've never heard of this kind of candy before," John said. "Or have I?"

"It's pretty good," Roger said. He unwrapped one and popped it into his mouth. "The flavor changes the longer it lasts."

"I'm already thirsty," John said. "But why not?"

John put the marble-sized candy in his mouth. He rolled it around with his tongue, then smiled.

"Not bad," he said.

"And it's free," Roger added. "You can't beat free."

"Let's go," John agreed. "This can wait."

"John," Susan said. But she could already see he was a lost cause. "I'm telling Dad if you go."

"He's not even here," John said. "But if he was, he'd understand."

"Mr. Fenster won't understand though," Susan shot back.

"The old goat can eat his grass for all I care," John said and laughed.

"I've already lost a whole truckload of toys listening to you. I'm not going to lose this chance too."

"I'll ride you on my bike," Roger said. "We need to hurry."

John straddled the front tire of his friend's bike, then pushed himself up so he was sitting on the handlebars. "Tell me if you see any cars coming," Roger said. "I can't see very well."

"Dad says you can't ride like that on someone else's bike," Susan warned. "You better stop it."

"You better start mowing and fast," John called to her. "You know how impatient old man Fenster is."

Both boys laughed as Roger pedaled away from the curb. Susan called after them. She knew they could hear her, but they just kept going. She was ready to throw down her hand clippers in anger, but then she saw Mr. Fenster looking out of the living room window at her.

Muttering under her breath, she yanked as hard as she could on the lawn-mower cord. The mower roared to life as the rope snapped. Susan sat down hard on the sidewalk, holding the broken cord. She jumped up to adjust the idle. John and Roger were already out of sight. "That's it," Susan said. "That's the straw that broke this camel's back." She pushed the mower up on the lawn and began to cut the long green grass, the broken pull cord still lying on the sidewalk.

Susan's mind seethed every step of the way as she pushed the lawn mower. And to make things worse, Mr. Fenster came outside to watch. That's when the mower stalled and quit. The old man walked over to complain while Susan tried to get the mower started.

Fortunately, Susan was a fairly good mechanic. She had replaced the pull cord before, but it still took time. Yet she felt like she was all thumbs with Mr. Fenster looking over her shoulder and sputtering about how long it was taking. Susan was ready to scream by the time she got the pull cord to finally work.

She worked as fast as she could after that. But Mr. Fenster had a big lawn. He stood with his hands on his hips the whole time, just frowning and watching her. Susan was burning inside, but she tried not to let it show.

When the grass was finally cut, Susan skipped her normal water break so she could begin clipping right away. That's when she saw John coming up the street. Mr. Fenster saw him too. The old man walked briskly to the front of his yard. He was pacing back and forth on the sidewalk when John arrived.

"Most boys finish a job they start," Mr. Fenster whined. "They don't go running off without telling someone."

"I had to do something," John said.

"And I've been waiting to water and plant some flowers all day too," Mr. Fenster said as if he didn't hear John. "You kids told me you'd be done by ten o'clock and it's almost eleven."

"I'm sorry," John said.

"Sorry won't get my petunias in the ground, will it?" Mr. Fenster demanded. "Just see that it doesn't happen again." The old man walked up his sidewalk and slammed the front door.

John went over to the hedge where Susan was clipping. Her face was red and streaked with sweat. She looked up at John, but didn't say anything, and went back to her clipping. "Boy, is Mr. Fenster a grouch," John said softly. "Need some help?"

"I needed some help about an hour ago," Susan said crisply. "Besides the mower breaking, I've had Mr. Fenster breathing down my neck the whole time."

"You know why I had to leave," John said defensively.

"Yeah, toys," Susan said. "Well, I hope you had a lot of fun."

"Actually, the whole thing was a waste of time," John said bitterly. "By the time we got there, half the kids in town were in line. And by then, Mrs. Happy was making everyone draw a number by chance. You won't believe what number I got. Five hundred and sixty-four. Can you believe it? I didn't know there were that many kids in Centerville."

"That's a real shame," Susan said flatly.

"If I could have just gotten there sooner, like Barry and his stupid club," John grunted. "They got the first seven numbers. Barry is Number One. While I was standing there in line they came to gloat too. They told Roger how they bombed us out at the dump. Then they even asked Roger if he wanted to join their club. Roger said no, but he did go over to Barry's house to play water basketball in the Smedlowe's pool. I can't believe he'd even hang out with those guys. I think Barry told Roger something about the toys at the dump too. I heard them whispering right before they all left. I'm beginning to wonder if I can trust Roger. If the Cobra Club gets those toys before I do, I think I'll die!"

Susan looked up at John and glared. The sweat dripped off her nose. John looked around the yard. He knew Susan was angry, but he felt she could at least be a little sympathetic about his bad luck at the toy store.

"Did you say something was wrong with the mower?" John asked finally. "Want me to fix it?"

"It's fixed," Susan said and stood up straight. "I don't need you. Just go on home. Or better yet, why don't you go out to the dump and look for your precious toys? I'm not working with you anymore. You are fired. I'll get another partner."

"Be that way then," John said.

Susan went back to her clipping. She didn't look up until the hedge was completely trimmed. By then John was gone.

THE
PARADE
BEGINS
· · · · · · · ·

15

July Fourth came to the town of Centerville at last. Susan woke up to the sound of firecrackers popping off in the distance. Someone was getting a head start on celebrating even though firecrackers were forbidden inside the town limits.

As sheriff, her father always had an especially busy day on the Fourth of July. But he had called around supper time the night before to say that he and her mom wouldn't be home until Saturday morning since the doctors wanted to run some additional tests. Susan had felt especially homesick when she talked to her father on the phone. She didn't think she could stand an extra day of Aunt Bernice. Susan walked slowly to the kitchen.

Katherine and Lois were making a special batch of blueberry and walnut pancakes at the stove. Aunt Bernice was helping them. John was setting the table. He ignored Susan. He had been in a bad mood ever since he had gotten the last number in the drawing for the toys. But that had just been the beginning of his bad luck. After Susan had fired him, he had gone home to get some gloves and a pick ax to dig for toys out at the dump.

But before he could leave, Aunt Bernice had recruited him to help her clean all the windows in the house. Then she had him work in the yard the rest of the afternoon, weeding the flower beds and digging dandelions out of the grass. If she didn't like the way he did a job, which was most of the time, she made him do it again. And if that wasn't bad enough, after supper she had made him clean his room and clean up the garage too.

By the time he had finished, it was too dark to go to the dump. He was calling her General Bernice under his breath by the time he went to bed. The whole miserable day had been lost, a day that he should have been digging for the toys in the dump.

The tasty smells of the pancakes and bacon that morning couldn't cheer John. He plopped the dishes down so hard that Aunt Bernice scolded him. "Well, I'm sorry," John said and sighed. He sat down.

"Morning," Aunt Bernice said to Susan, wiping her hands on her apron.

"G'morning!" Susan replied flatly.

"What a dreary bunch of children you are," Aunt Bernice said. "And on a holiday too. My Cecilia and Clarence loved the Fourth of July almost as much as Christmas. It's a day to celebrate freedom."

"Why should we be happy?" John asked. "We're all at the end of the line. I still can't believe it. Out of all the kids in the whole town, our family gets the last four numbers. How can that happen? It's like she planned it."

"It does seem unusual," Aunt Bernice said as she watched Lois pour out a circle of batter onto the hot skillet. "But it was a drawing. That's just the way things happen sometimes. Besides, it's not the end of the world. And when you get free gifts, you don't have any right to be choosy."

"I bet it'll just be a bunch of junk anyway," Susan said. Susan hadn't picked a number card herself because she had been too busy cutting lawns and trimming by herself. Lois had picked a number for her.

"She couldn't really afford to give away nice toys anyway," Lois said.

"We'll never get one even if she did," John whined. "Not with five hundred and sixty-one kids ahead of us. If I weren't mowing lawns all the time, I could have gotten there early like Roger and got in the top one hundred."

"Well, you won't have to worry about that anymore," Susan commented.

"You children have a nice little business," Aunt Bernice said. "And you have plenty of free time too. My Cecilia and Clarence used to work much harder than you two. Kids today don't know the meaning of work."

"And just think of the line," John moaned. "It'll be ten blocks long, I bet."

"At least you'll know your place in the line," Lois offered. "Right there at the very end. And you can look for us."

"I'm not even going to stand in line," Susan said. "At least not until there's only a few people left."

"That sounds like a wise idea," Aunt Bernice replied. She flipped three pancakes over. "You won't waste any time that way."

"Can I flip a pancake?" Lois asked.

"Sure. This one's almost ready," Aunt Bernice replied, pointing to one. "Turn it when you see lots of little bubbles in the batter."

"Some of the blueberries look like bubbles," Lois said, staring at the pancake. She stood on a stool.

"I heard a bunch of kids were going over to the Smedlowe's house to swim and eat stuff today after they get their free toys," Susan said. "I think even some of my friends may go."

"I bet Roger will go too," John said bitterly. "I can't believe he'd even think twice about making friends with that guy. Roger stopped by while I was digging dandelions yesterday. He said the Dead Men's Club talked about Mrs. Happy and some weird plan she has to stop an 'enemy invasion' in Centerville. None of it made much sense to me. She's supposed to do something special at the fireworks show tonight."

"Enemy invasion?" Lois asked. "You mean there's going to be some kind of war?"

"I don't think so. It all sounded very strange," John said. "I don't know what he meant. He said the free toys were connected to her plan somehow. But then he acted real secretive about the whole thing. Roger isn't usually like that."

"It doesn't sound good to me," Susan said after a pause. "I wonder if Mrs. Happy has some scheme in mind. I'm not sure we should take her toys. And didn't you say something about fireworks yesterday, John, when we talked about when you disappeared?"

But before John could answer, Aunt Bernice interrupted, "Toys are for having fun, child, not for fighting."

"I'm not so sure," Susan responded. She could think of a lot of toys that were made for war and violence.

"Well, breakfast is ready," Aunt Bernice said cheerfully.

Susan and John barely finished a pancake apiece. His heart wasn't in it. All he could think about was that he would be the last person in a very long line.

Susan was ready for her parents to be home, and she couldn't shake her uneasy feelings about the toy store. Even though blueberry and walnut pancakes were one of her favorites, she barely picked at the food on her plate. Nothing tasted good.

The Happy Toy Store was scheduled to open at eleven o'clock, right after the parade. Like almost every other kid in town, Susan found herself walking downtown toward the store around 9:00. The parade began at 9:30. Trying to resist the pull of her curiosity, Susan made a detour by the town park to watch the goings-on. There were banners stretched between the light poles. The old bandstand was covered with red, white and blue bunting. The town parade was being formed up just off South Main Street, four blocks from the town square.

Every year Centerville had a small but nice parade. The school band led the way, followed by antique cars with the town council and mayor and other city officials. As Mr. Kramar liked to say, half the town watched the other half march in the parade. Some children dressed up as clowns and others twirled batons. Almost anyone who wanted to march could be in the parade. Some years people rode their horses. Many children decorated their bicycles and rode together. The town volunteer fire department always came last. They drove the new and old fire engines and blew the siren to signal that the parade was over.

After the parade, the band would set up in the bandstand and give a short concert. The town square was usually packed and people had a lot of fun. In the evening the band played again out on the athletic field at the school. After that, the fire department set off the fireworks display.

When Susan saw so many of the children heading for the toy store, she couldn't resist any longer. She joined the crowd and followed. Main Street was blocked off because of the parade. But even Susan wasn't prepared for the sight of so many children wandering around the toy store. The new signs and the sight of all the toys had made everyone more excited than ever.

Just then, John and Roger walked up behind her. Susan turned around. "This is worse than I thought," John said to Roger, looking over at the blinking purple sign.

"I tried to get up by the front door, but it was impossible," Roger said. "People were pushing and shoving. I heard there were boxes of free candy up there. And you won't guess who is giving it out."

"Who?" John asked.

"Barry and the Cobra Club," Roger said. "I guess since they're the first ones in line, she's letting them give out the candy. I had Bruce get me a bunch. He's number twelve. You want some?"

"Sure," John said. Roger gave John a handful of Sweet Temptations. John popped one into his mouth. "I bet there won't be any good stuff left by the time I get there."

"I still can't believe your family picked the last four numbers," Roger told his friend sympathetically.

"It's like we're cursed or something," John said, shaking his head.

"We aren't cursed," Susan said, disgusted by all the commotion around her.

"Well, it does seem unlucky," Roger said.

"We might as well leave," John said, looking at Susan. "I've been thinking of riding a bike in the parade this year. Do you want to? I heard Bruce and Rick might."

"I don't know," Roger said. "I want to be sure and get a good place in line. Even though I have number seventeen, people might try to cheat anyway. You can't be too careful."

"Maybe so," said John. He wanted his friend to ride with him in the parade, but he didn't want to show his disappointment. "I just hope there are some good toys left."

"I'm not even sure you guys should take her toys," Susan warned. "It seems all these rumors of an enemy invasion are connected to the free toys somehow. The whole thing seems suspicious to me, and so does Mrs. Happy."

"I have no idea what you have against toys. First it's the dump, and now it's this. Let's go, Roger," John said. And with that, the two boys walked away. More and more children were filling the street. Susan wondered if there would be room for the parade to pass by.

Inside the store, Mrs. Happy was busy setting up a large black box. It was taller than she was and appeared to be made of a the same shiny material as the mysterious black window on her desk. On the front side there was a large white circle with an X on the inside. At the center of the X was a hole about the size of a soccer ball. The rest of the sides were plain black, without markings. On the back side was a square hole with a small chute sticking out.

The old woman looked inside the hole in the middle of the circled X, then smiled. "Everything is prepared," she said to the black crow perched up on top of the cash register. "All according to the book. The Bureau should be delighted with this operation. Of course, I will get results, unlike you, noodlehead. The Bureau knows that."

The crow fluttered his wings. "I tried," the bird said in his small voice.

"And you failed, that's why you got demoted to the birdbrain you are," Mrs. Happy said. "To go from an R-17 all the way down to Z-4. What an embarrassment. You should thank your lucky ashes that you're not on your belly permanently."

The crow flew up on the toy shelf closest to the door. The cold black eyes stared at the big front windows of the store. Over fifty small faces were pressed against the glass, trying to see all the toys inside.

"They call this their Independence Day," Mrs. Happy said to the crow, then laughed. "They should call it 'All Fools Day.' It's perfect for starting the Toy Campaign. The hunger of the children is ripe as rotting fruit. But we'll give them what they want, and even more, won't we? They'll get their trinkets, and tonight I'll get my signatures, and then they'll be in our grasp. The little fools are so predictable."

Nail bobbed his little head up and down.

"One step at a time," Mrs. Happy said. "The Bureau has used this plan thousands of times. We won't yield an inch. And they never feel a thing. It's like they're asking for the chains to be tightened."

"The girl, the girl," Nail said. "Don't forget the girl."

"She's not a threat anymore," the old woman said. "She's feeding on her spite and self-pity like a kitten laps up milk. And by the time we're through, she'll wish she never heard the name Spirit Flyer. She'll learn to respect the pull of the chain and the point of the hook, just like her miserable cousin John."

Mrs. Happy chuckled to herself. A bowl full of a gray powder rested on the counter top next to the cash register. She stuck her hand into the bowl and scooped up a handful of the powder. She held the ashes up to her mouth, then poured them in.

Outside, a siren blasted a short wail. The children wandering around outside on Main Street moved toward the sidewalks. A drum boomed and a clarinet squeaked.

"Independence Day," Mrs. Happy said to the bird. "The parade of the puppets is about to begin." And with that, she made sure she was smiling and walked toward the front of the store. One hand gripped several dark hooks. The children cheered when they saw her open the door.

TOY
FEVER
• • • • • • • •
16

Barry Smedlowe and the Cobra Club
shoved their way past a group of baton twirlers. The boys were dressed
in black pants and wore their black jackets with the picture on the back
of a cobra ready to strike.

"I don't see why we have to be in the parade," Doug complained. "I
want to be ready when Happy Toys opens."

"We're the first in line, you dummy," Barry said. "Can't you count to
seven yet?"

"Are you sure she won't start without us?" Doug asked.

"You heard her say she won't just ten minutes ago," Barry said. "Now
quit complaining, and don't drop your end of the banner. I want to show

the town who's Number One."

Doug and Jimmy held up the banner. Slashed across the banner in black paint were the words:

Cobra Club!!!

Join the Fun. Be Number One!!!

"This will let the kids in town know who we are," Barry said. "Join us and have fun. We'll make them pay dues. We'll clean up!"

"Not so loud," Doug whispered. "And besides, how do you know they'll pay dues and join up?"

"They'll pay if they want to play," Barry said. "No pay, no play. Simple."

"I don't know," Doug said doubtfully. "A lot of kids think that you're . . . well, you know what some of the other kids say, not that I would say those things."

"You better not!" Barry warned. Then he remembered to smile his new, improved smile. He slapped Doug on the back like a buddy. "Trust me. By the end of the summer, we'll be living like kings. I've got it all figured out. Now let's go!"

The Cobra Club members cheered and pushed their way up closer to the front of the parade, right behind the mayor's old antique car. Barry rode in front and then Doug and Jimmy stretched the banner between themselves behind him. The rest of the gang followed.

When John Kramar rode up on the Goliath bicycle, the band had already begun to play. John looked for other friends on bicycles in the parade. He didn't see anyone but Barry's group. Then he saw Susan, Lois and Katherine sitting on their Spirit Flyers. John rode over.

"Not many kids are riding in the parade this year," John said.

"Everyone's worried about losing their place in line at the toy store," Susan said. "It's crazy. That's all anyone can talk about. The parade won't be nearly as nice. Mr. Brooks was yelling at the band because a whole bunch of the older kids didn't even want to play. If you ask me, this Grand Opening Day Celebration is going to ruin the parade."

"Well, this is the first time we've had a Grand Opening Celebration at the toy store," Lois said. "And it's new and improved besides. Don't you want to be happy, like the picture says? I do. I want to be just like that happy girl with Happy Toys."

"She doesn't care whether you're happy or not. She'll be happy because she'll be making all the money in a few days. I don't think we should take her toys, Lois. I don't think they'll be good for our Spirit Flyers."

"You're just mad because we're the last ones in line," Lois said.

"I am not," Susan said.

"I'm going to the toy store just as soon as this dumb old parade is over," Lois said. Even if we are last, I want to see what toys my friends get."

"Me too," added Katherine in her tiny voice.

The band began to play. A few bicycles joined the parade near the end, right in front of the fire engines. Susan and the others rode over to join them.

The parade started up South Main Street before it circled around the square. Everything looked about the same as the year before, except that more children were just watching the parade than being in it. The children and grownups were on the sidewalks, and when the band passed, they cheered and clapped.

The marches the band played always stirred Susan's heart too. Though she and the few other bicycle riders were farther back, they could still hear the old familiar tunes. Susan liked the trombones the best. She planned to learn to play one when she returned to school in the fall. Her sisters liked the big drums and cymbals.

As the parade passed in front of Happy Toys, many of the children in the band looked over hopefully at the big windows. The lights had been turned on so they could see the rows and rows of bright shiny toys. The two big pictures of the contented boy and girl looked back at all the children of the town. If you looked at the pictures long enough, you could almost begin to see your face in the picture as the happy boy or girl. Many children found it hard to look away. Mrs. Happy was on the front step. She smiled and waved at the children in the band. The big purple sign blinked on and off.

Even though the parade was only half over when it passed the toy store, many children in the parade stopped marching and joined the growing line on the sidewalk. Each child was showing the next child his or her number. Some children began to argue. Mrs. Happy didn't seem to mind. She smiled at everyone.

"Just find your place in line," she said to the children who came running up. "There's plenty of toys for one and all."

More and more children left the Independence Day parade as they saw the other children leaving. When the Cobra Club passed by and saw the line forming, some members became worried.

"I think we should get our place now," Doug hissed at Barry.

"Yeah," Jimmy added.

"She won't start without us," Barry said. "I want to show everyone who we are."

The grownups noticed the children crowding up around the toy store, but no one said anything. Those children who had to stay with their parents were begging to leave.

"Hardly anyone's paying attention to the parade," Susan said to Lois as they rolled slowly down Main Street. Three of the bicycle riders in front of Susan sprinted out of their place and jumped their bikes up on the sidewalk. They pedaled straight for the toy store as fast as they could go.

By the time Susan passed the toy store, only six other bike riders remained. Mrs. Happy looked carefully at Susan and John. She smiled and waved. Most children were comparing their numbers instead of looking at the parade anymore. Some children were yelling, a few were shoving.

Far up the street, the head of the parade reached the square. But instead of turning to march around the block, some of the children at the rear of the band began to run back toward the toy store. Then suddenly, the whole band began to run at once.

"Look, it's a stampede!" Susan cried as she saw the band members in their bright red uniforms running against the flow of the parade.

The sight of the running band members did it. Suddenly there were two parades going in opposite directions. The Independence Day parade was falling apart. Toy fever burned in every child's heart. Each child that had been wanting to leave, got up and ran with the crowd. Even the children of the mayor and town council members hopped out of the antique automobiles and ran back toward the toy store. The street clogged with children. Every child in town was moving toward the toy store as if being pulled on a string. The Independence Day parade disappeared in the crowded confusion.

The line was forming on the sidewalk, but not without much arguing and shoving. There was a sea of hands holding up the black plastic numbers. Everyone was sure that someone else was cutting in line. The shoving got worse. John saw a first-grade girl get knocked down on the sidewalk. The noise was deafening.

The firetrucks couldn't move through the crowd. "This parade is over," Chief Bloomer said, shaking his head. "Let her blow."

The fire sirens began to wail. That began to quiet the children, but not too much. Deputy Baker arrived in the police car, his red and blue lights flashing. The children stopped shoving when they saw him coming. Barry Smedlowe and the Cobra Club were right behind the police car.

"Out of my way. We're Number One," Barry said. "Out of our way. Police escort. Move it. The line starts behind me!"

Main Street began to clear as the police car came down the street. The fighting and yelling stopped. A little girl and two little boys were crying. The car stopped in front of the Happy Toy Store. Deputy Baker got out. Before he could speak, Barry Smedlowe and the Cobra Club pushed

their way up to the door of the toy store. Barry parked his bike in the street, then held up his number.

"Number One right here," Barry said. "Move away from that door. The line starts behind me and my club. We have numbers one through seven."

"I've never seen such a mess," Deputy Baker said to Mrs. Happy. "Ok. Line up. And no pushing."

"Please let ten children in at a time, officer," Mrs. Happy said to Deputy Baker. She smiled, then went inside the store. Barry and the Cobra Club were right behind her, but she closed the door in their faces. Deputy Baker and several grownups tried to get the children to form a line. Mr. Smedlowe stomped up to the deputy.

"Why isn't this situation under control?" Mr. Smedlowe demanded. "We almost had a wreck with four trumpet players and my antique Ford Model T. I think some paint might have gotten chipped on that car. I'm holding the police department responsible."

"Why don't you give us a hand here? You're the school principal," Deputy Baker said, trying not to show his anger. "With the sheriff gone, it's harder to keep order. Nobody expected a mess like this."

"I guess somebody around here has to take charge," Mr. Smedlowe snorted. "Here. You, boy. What's your number? Thirty-three? Can't you count? You're standing between twenty-five and twenty-six. Get back where you belong."

"That's Don Wilburn and Martha Grimes," Deputy Baker said. "Why don't you use their names?"

"Let's just get this over and done with, shall we, Deputy?" Mr. Smedlowe grunted. "All I see is numbers. And numbers out of order at that. What's your number, boy? Stop that shoving . . ."

Far down the street, Susan and Lois and Katherine watched the mob of children fighting for their place in line. John had gotten lost somewhere in the crowd. Susan shook her head.

"Can you believe it?" she asked. "I thought I was going to get run over by those two big tuba players."

"Mary is even bigger with her tuba," Katherine said, nodding.

"I was riding along next to Cynthia," Lois said, "and she knocked me and my Spirit Flyer right down on the sidewalk when all the kids started running."

"I just tried to get out of the way," Susan said. "Someone bent the rear fender, I think."

"It was bent anyway," Katherine replied. "What a mess."

"Poor Mr. Baker," Susan said. "I bet he wishes Daddy were here to help."

"I wanted to watch, but I think I'm going home to wait," Lois said. "Here comes John."

John pushed his black bicycle out of the crowd and headed toward the town square. "I was almost squashed," he said as he came up to the others.

"We're going home to wait," Katherine said. "Are you coming, John?"

"I've got other plans," John said. "And I don't want General Bernice to see me. She messed me up yesterday, but she's not going to mess me up today. She'd have me washing the sidewalk with a toothbrush if she got the chance."

"We can come back after lunch," Lois said to Katherine and Susan. "The line will have gone down by then."

"I don't think any of us should go," urged Susan. "I'm afraid there could be some danger."

"Oh, you don't know what's going on in there," Lois said.

"Well, I know what I'm going to do," John said, hitting his leg with his fist. "I'm getting my toys early. And I know just where to go."

"You aren't going back out to the dump, are you?" Susan asked.

As an answer, John turned the Goliath Cobra Deluxe around. Susan was right behind him. They were going fast by the time they sped down the alley behind the toy store. Neither one looked back at the long line of children moving slowly into the store like a parade of puppets.

MRS.
HAPPY'S
PUPPETS
· · · · · · · ·
17

"Step right up to this box," Mrs. Happy said.
Barry Smedlowe and the first nine children were inside the toy store at
last. Mrs. Happy took them over to the big black box right away.

"Everyone takes a turn," the old woman instructed. "Put your number
in this slot here and your face up to this hole. The box will take your
number. Then there will be a flash, like someone taking a photograph.
After that flash, move aside for the next child. Walk around to the other
side of the box and you will receive your number again and your first
toy."

Barry and the other children gazed around at all the toys. Barry stepped up to the box. "What kind of toy is it?" Barry asked.

"Don't ask questions. There are a lot of children waiting," Mrs. Happy said. "Just do as I say, then wait for me over at those big shelves by the cash register."

Barry shrugged his shoulders, then stepped up to the large black box. He stared at the white circled X, then put his face in the hole. The blue flash blinded him for an instant. As the box began to hum, Barry walked to the other side. In a few seconds, the black plastic number and a small gray figure fell out of the chute onto the floor. Barry picked up both.

"Hey, it's me," the bigger boy said with delight. "It's a sort of puppet, but it has my face. Look, it has little chains instead of strings on the arms and legs. And my face is on the number card now too. Only it's kind of dark. It's right in the plastic."

"It's a perfect likeness, now move along," Mrs. Happy said. She snatched the puppet out of his hands and tossed it into a large metal bin behind the black box. "The puppet belongs to me, or rather, the Goliath Toy Company. Who's next?"

"I am," Jimmy Roundhouse said, holding up the number two.

"Ok, Two, step up to the box," Mrs. Happy said. "Many children are waiting."

Jimmy Roundhouse stepped up to the big black box. He put in his number, then stuck his face in the hole. The blue light flashed like a bolt of lightning. Jimmy walked around to the back. His number and another gray puppet fell out of the chute onto the floor.

"This one has my face too," Jimmy said. "What a crazy box."

"Hurry along, children," Mrs. Happy said. "Put your puppets in the bin, but keep your number card. That's the rule. I have more surprises."

"What are those puppets good for?" Barry asked.

"Just hold onto to your number card and do as I say," Mrs. Happy replied cheerfully. "Hurry, children. Others are waiting. It's your turn, Number Three."

Each child stepped up to the big black box like the one before. Mrs.

Happy smiled at the sight. In a few minutes, the first ten children all had pictures of their faces on the number cards. Each of the puppet faces were frozen in a big toothy smile.

"Now come over to these shelves," Mrs. Happy said, as she stepped over to the cash register. Just then, Nail the crow flew over to Mrs. Happy's shoulder. The bird put its beak into the old woman's ear and began whispering.

"You saw who going down the alley?" Mrs. Happy asked. A frown appeared on the old woman's face as she listened some more. "Then you know what to do. They must be processed like the rest."

"Excuse me," the old woman said. She walked over to the front door and opened it. A cheer came up from the crowd. Nail flew up into the air. Everyone groaned when the door shut in their faces. The old woman walked back over to the group of ten children.

"You may take two of any toy on these shelves," Mrs. Happy said. "But choose carefully."

Barry looked at the long row of shelves. It was full of brand new toys, but toys that were somehow slightly different than most toys. "I've never seen toys like these," Barry said. "What are they?"

"Gather round, children," Mrs. Happy said. "I suppose I shall be explaining these toys all day. But since they are special and come new and improved from the Goliath Toy Company, I will tell you what they are. Then you can choose."

The children crowded up around the shelves of the strange new toys. Barry was in front of them all.

"First you can have a ball," Mrs. Happy said. "What's a child without a ball? We have all the standard ones, of course. We have the regular Goliath Ball, then we have Soot Ball, Slammer Ball, Odd Ball, Zip Ball, Zero Ball, Slime Ball and Bopper Ball. Plus to go with those we have Smacker Paddles and Zatbats. We also carry Boomerringers and Zicky-Stickies."

The children whispered among themselves. Barry reached out slowly and touched a Soot ball carefully. His finger came back with a black smudge.

"Don't touch that Soot Ball unless you plan to take it," Mrs. Happy warned. "We have all Goliath brand dolls too, including the popular elvish dolls, Snout, Pouty and Cork. We also carry old favorites like Sissy Sassy, Woozy Soozy, the twins Peedledum and Peedledee, Dimply Pimply, Honey Runny, the Null Doll (also know as 2Face) and Ginny Goo Goo. Ginny comes in the popular Gooseberry scent. Your mother will almost want to make a pie out of her."

"Make a pie to eat from a doll?" asked Cynthia, who was number nine. Mrs. Happy ignored her.

"Then we have all kinds of noisemakers," the old woman said. "These will really make your parents sit up and notice you. We have Tickletones, Screambones, Zootones, Clamorfones, Follytones, Hoobas, Poppersings, Fingerblows, Doodlesnits, Teeterkeys, Blahfones, Yakfones and Zingos."

"That Fingerblow looks like a tiny bagpipe," Brent said. He was number four.

"Hush, child," Mrs. Happy said. "Then we have all kinds of Goliath Monster Action Figures like Blackeye, Bait, Bite, Boil, Chainsaw, Sore, Greenie, Bullet, Razor, Thief, Nuke, Mute and Rat. A whole set of Goliath Action Victims are coming in next week, including the popular Kazoombies."

"It looks like my dog Sparky used ol' Bait there for a dog chew," Alvin said. He was number seven.

"And then we have just general fun stuff," Mrs. Happy said. "Like Square skates, Sucker stickers and accessories, Bop-Bots, Claw-Bots, Robber-Bots, Zebdogs, Toetrippers, Teddybites, Ripzippers, Face-erase, Goliath Dice, the Goliath Credit Bank, Sting strings, Whippersnaps, Stop-n-Start Darts, which of course includes the Zing-bow to shoot them."

A girl picked up a Teddybite. It looked like a fuzzy teddy bear that was scowling. She smiled at the odd bear and its jaws snapped down on her finger. She threw it back on the shelf.

"Don't touch it unless you plan to own one," Mrs. Happy said. "They don't like to be touched by just anybody. You must have activated its batteries. Now, let's see. We have a few special things for your bicycle. Like a Goliath Combo-Gizmo and a Faster Blaster. There are some other things that still haven't come in from the factory, but these should keep you occupied."

The children stared at the odd-looking toys without a word. They had never seen such toys. Then at last, Barry was the one to break the silence.

"Is that all there is?" the leader of the Cobra Club asked. Barry looked unhappy.

"Why don't you consider the bicycle toys?" Mrs. Happy asked. "I would recommend them for someone in your position. They attach to your bike and do wonderful things."

"Like what?" Barry asked. He picked up a strange-looking toy. It had a dial and buttons and a kind of gauge that looked like a speedometer. It also had two little wires shooting out the top like a TV antenna.

"Excellent choice," Mrs. Happy said. "That's a marvelous toy. That's the ever-popular Goliath Combo-Gizmo. It goes on your bicycle. It has a speeder-meter, a zero radio, part walkie-talkie and a shock screen."

"Really?" Barry asked. "Does it come with an earphone too?"

"Yes, of course," Mrs. Happy said. "With a Combo-Gizmo, you can be wired up to secretly listen to all your favorite noises and so forth."

"I'll take it," Barry said. He clutched the Combo-Gizmo in his hands.

"Just remember that to make it work, you need to put your number card in this little slot here," Mrs. Happy said. "Without your number card, it won't work. And of course you need two batteries. They aren't included."

"No batteries," Barry asked. "I knew there was a catch." The president of the Cobra Club looked at the shelves of toys. "I want something that will really be fun."

"What kind of fun?" Mrs. Happy asked and smiled.

"You know, really fun," Barry said.

"My boy, there are many types of fun in this world," Mrs. Happy said. "You'll have to be more specific."

Barry looked confused. His forehead wrinkled as he thought. "You know, really fun fun," Barry said. "Like when you throw water balloons at someone or on Halloween when you soap windows and smash pumpkins."

"That's better," Mrs. Happy said. "I know the kind of fun you mean. Of course Halloween is too far away, which is too bad. We have some really great toys and costumes for Halloween. But what I think you'd like is this Goliath Faster Blaster. It will fit right on your handlebars next to your Combo-Gizmo."

She pulled out a black plastic toy that looked like a machine gun. She gave it to the boy.

"That's more like it," Barry said. "But what does it shoot?"

"Whatever you aim it at, I suppose," Mrs. Happy said.

"No, I mean what kind of ammunition does it shoot?" Barry asked. "Is it one of those motorized water guns or something like that?"

"It will shoot water and many other things, like Zammo-ammo, for instance," Mrs. Happy said. "All Goliath ammunition works in a Faster Blaster. I've been told even Stop-n-Start Darts will work, but I can't guarantee it."

"Can I get some of that Zammo stuff too?" Barry asked.

"Sorry," Mrs. Happy said. "Ammunition is not included. You'll have to pretend for right now. Or you could work up enough credit for the Stop-n-Start Darts. I haven't received any Zammo-ammo pellets from Goliath Toys yet. And remember, you'll need your number card to get the right ammo for your toy. These are special toys and you must have your number card."

"You mean I need the number card to buy more stuff?" Barry asked.

"That's correct," replied Mrs. Happy. "You need the number card to buy. And you also need the number card to make many of the toys work. And on top of that, you need Goliath Credit."

"You mean this is like a credit card?" Barry asked.

"Of course," Mrs. Happy said. "So don't lose it."

"I'll take the Faster Blaster," Barry said. "I sure wish the ammo was in, though."

"Another good choice," the old woman said. "Now run along and let the others have their turn."

Jimmy Roundhouse had been listening to what Mrs. Happy had been telling Barry. "I want the same toys," Jimmy said.

"Excellent," Mrs. Happy said. "Another Goliath Combo-Gizmo and a Goliath Faster Blaster coming up. Remember to hold onto your number card. These toys won't work properly without it."

Barry went out the front door. The line of children all strained to see what Barry was carrying.

"Hurry up, Number Three," Mrs. Happy called to the next boy.

"What'd you get, Barry?" a boy named Timmy Bellows asked. He was number sixteen, right in front of Roger.

"A Goliath Combo-Gizmo and a Goliath Faster Blaster," Barry said.

"Can I see them?" another boy asked. "I never heard of toys like that."

"Get your own," Barry said. "I'm busy." He got on his bike and waited for his friends. Jimmy came out next, then Doug and the rest of the Cobra Club. They all had the same identical toys. The other children waiting in line wanted to see, but the Cobra Club stuck together.

"Let's go," Barry said. He held up his Faster Blaster in one arm and waved it forward like a soldier leading a charge. The other boys hooted and yelled at those remaining in line as they pedaled down Main Street.

Mr. Smedlowe sent in the next group of ten children as the Numbers Eight, Nine and Ten came out with their free toys.

"Step right up to the big black box, Number Eleven," Mrs. Happy said. "And make sure you hang on to your number card. You'll need to keep it to use with some of the toys. You also will need it to make future orders. Put the card in the slot, and your face up to the window. There will be a flash, like a photograph. Then go around to the back. Put the puppet in the metal bin with the other puppets. They belong to me. And be sure to hang on to that number card . . ."

"I told you going back to the dump would be a mistake," Susan was telling John. Her cousin was red-faced and angry as he sat on the back of her Spirit Flyer bicycle.

But John wasn't listening. He had hoped he could get the buried toys at the dump while the line at the toy store got shorter. After much digging, he had uncovered a box he was sure was full of toys. But that's when the Cobra Club had showed up. Under Barry's command the boys had shot firecrackers and cherry bombs with their new Faster Blasters. And when John tried to escape, he discovered that the Cobra Club had also stolen his Goliath bike. He was trapped and would have been in serious trouble if Susan hadn't zoomed in out of the sky to rescue him.

Susan had landed the bike at the bridge over the Sleepy Eye River. John felt frustrated that he had just missed getting the toys again. And letting the Cobra Club capture his Goliath bike was pure humiliation. Susan felt sorry for John.

As the two children looked back in the direction of the dump, they saw smoke rising in the air. Apparently the firecrackers had started something burning. "Well, at least I can still get toys from Mrs. Happy," John said as he pulled out his plastic card with five hundred sixty-four on it. He looked at it and then sighed. "Let's go back and check on the line." John began walking toward town.

Susan watched him in disbelief. Another try to get toys in the dump. Another attack. Another rescue. Still John had learned nothing. She stared at him for a long time trying to decide what to do. But John started running and was soon out of sight.

Susan looked back in the direction of the dump once more. As she turned to go back into town, she looked down at the old broken mirror.

This time the mirror showed the line at the toy store earlier that morning. Her eyes went wide with surprise. She stopped. She squinted and looked again. She stared back in time in a deeper way for several minutes. Now she knew how important it was to keep John and Lois and Katherine from getting their free toys.

"I've got to find them," Susan said. She looked back at the old mirror once more. This time the scene shifted. There was a mountain of toys with fireworks going off all around. And Mrs. Happy was there, and so was John, scooping up the toys in his arms. All the children in town were there, linked together by a long chain. Suddenly, all the pieces fell into place for Susan. She could see the future and she had to stop it. Immediately she began pedaling fast as she could go. The crow circling high above her swooped down closer. The little black eyes of the bird followed her all through town.

LOSING
A BATTLE

· · · · · · · ·

18

Susan thought it would be a simple task to warn her sisters and John about the dangers she had seen in the old mirror. But first she had to find them.

She thought for sure they would be at the toy store. She waited patiently across the street for more than a half-hour. But as the line of children got smaller and smaller, Susan grew more worried. When the last ten children went inside the mysterious toy store, Susan began to feel frightened. She wondered if her sisters and cousin had already gone through the line somehow.

She pedaled up and down Main Street, and let her worries grow.

Without thinking, or letting the Spirit Flyer lead, she rode home in a panic. But there was no one home, not even Aunt Bernice.

"I've got to get back to the toy store," Susan mumbled to herself. Deep inside she felt like she had made a big mistake by leaving. She pedaled back toward the toy store as fast as she could go. She had to keep those toys away from John and her sisters. She never thought to look up or she would have seen the crow flying overhead, following her like a tiny shadow.

While Susan sped down Tenth Street toward the town square, Barry Smedlowe and the Cobra Club had just ridden out of the alley behind the toy store. He popped a Sweet Temptation into his mouth and saw Susan coming down the street.

"Load up," Barry said. He pointed toward the girl. Barry and the Cobra Club hid behind a parked pickup truck and waited. The big boy was eager for revenge, but he was also a little scared. The mysterious powers of the old Spirit Flyer bicycles worried him.

"These Faster Blasters are great," Jimmy said. "I've never had so much fun."

"Mrs. Happy said they'll shoot even more stuff," Barry said. "She mentioned some kind of new ammunition was coming soon."

"I think they work great already," Alvin said. "Just blasting John Kramar out at the dump was good enough for me. And capturing his bike was even more fun."

"You think it's safe to shoot these in town?" Robert asked. Though he liked shooting the Faster Blasters, he was nervous because the fire-crackers made such a loud noise. The other boys seemed to like the risk.

"Here comes the target now," Barry said. All the boys looked. Susan Kramar was barreling up the street. Doug began to laugh. "Quiet!" Barry hissed. "We'll shoot just like before. Wait for my signal."

Susan hoped she wasn't too late. She pedaled faster. But just as she got to the corner of the town square, she heard a tiny blowing horn. "What now?" she asked out loud. She didn't want to stop, but she knew the horn might be warning her of something. She stepped on the brake.

"She's stopping," Doug whispered. They were all peeking out from behind the parked pickup.

"She can't have seen us," Barry whispered.

"Then why did she stop?" Jimmy asked.

"I don't know," the bigger boy said. "I'll count to three, and then we charge. We'll use the long fuses this time."

The boys quickly changed ammunition, keeping an eye on the girl.

The horn was still softly blowing. Susan cocked her head, then looked around. "I wonder why it's blowing when I . . ."

The Cobra Club shot out from behind the truck and headed straight for Susan. She saw the black instruments on the boy's bicycles. Then she noticed the flames of their lighters. "Strike!" the boys yelled and stood up on their pedals to go faster.

Susan crossed the street, racing toward the bandstand. The boys had gained a lot of speed by then. Susan jumped her bike up on the sidewalk. The Cobra Club jumped their bikes right behind her and cut across the corner just in front of the bandstand trying to head her off. The fuses sparkled and sputtered.

Susan looked over her shoulder. The boys were grinning with satisfaction knowing they were within range. Just then, three children stepped onto the sidewalk in front of Susan. She swerved off to the left going onto the grass. Barry smiled seeing that a row of rose bushes would stop the fleeing girl. Susan turned sharply in front of the racing bikes as she headed for the roses.

"Strike!" Barry yelled. But as the boys squeezed the triggers of their Faster Blasters, Susan pushed down on her handlebars. The old red bike soared up into the air as the Faster Blasters shot. The firecrackers exploded beneath her feet as she sailed over the row of bushes. The members of the Cobra Club tried to turn their bicycles, but they were going too fast. They were so surprised at the sight of her zooming over the roses, they forgot to brake in time for the hedge.

Susan heard their yells and the sound of metal hitting metal. She aimed the old red bicycle for the ground and landed gently. She wanted to look back at the wreck, but remembered that she needed to warn John and the others. She stood up on the pedals of the Spirit Flyer and shot across the grass.

She turned onto Main Street and slowed down for three passing cars. Then she pedaled down the block toward the toy store as fast as she could go. But her heart sank as she hopped off the bike. John came out of the toy store with two toys, followed by Lois and Katherine. Each of the girls also had two toys. They smiled when they saw Susan. All three were sucking on a fresh piece of green candy. Susan was crushed.

"Remember to hang on to those number cards," Mrs. Happy said. "They're important. And look who's arrived. The last number herself."

"John, you didn't take those toys, did you?" Susan asked, trying to catch her breath. "Give them back, quick. Before it's too late."

"Too late for what?" John asked. "These look pretty neat. Why would I want to give them back? I got a Goliath Combo-Gizmo and a Goliath Faster Blaster. These are the same toys Barry and his club got this morning, and they were the very first ones in line."

"No, no," Susan said. "They're not good toys. They'll ruin your Spirit Flyers. Give them back."

"Don't be silly, young lady," Mrs. Happy said. "Goliath Toys are of the finest quality."

"No, they're not, and you know it," Susan said fiercely to the old woman. Mrs. Happy looked coldly at Susan for a moment. Then her face brightened.

"I'm sorry you're upset, my child," Mrs. Happy said. "Your brother was upset too because he thought all the good toys would be gone. Many children have been thinking that all day long, yet they left happy and pleased with their free gifts. Come inside with your number. Just step up to the big black box. There will be a flash like someone taking your picture . . ."

"Here's your number card, Susan," Lois said, giving her sister the black piece of plastic. "You were the very last one, number five hundred and sixty-five. I brought it from home for you. You put it in the big black box."

"That's when it makes a funny puppet," Katherine said. "Both the number card and the puppet had my face on it."

"I'm not taking anything of yours," Susan said to the old woman. "Keep your number." Susan threw the black plastic number at Mrs. Happy. The old woman blinked in surprise as the number hit her and fell on the ground.

"Susan!" John said in surprise. He had never known her to be so rude. Mrs. Happy continued to smile as she bent down to pick up the number.

"Come see for yourself, my child, if you think . . ."

"I don't want to see anything," Susan said. "You tricked John and my sisters and probably the whole town for that matter, but you don't fool me. You don't fool me about tonight either."

"No one is fooling anyone, my dear," Mrs. Happy said. "Every child in town is happy now, playing with his or her new toys. They've become part of the Goliath Toy family. And it's one big happy family as you will see if you just take your number and step up to the big box. You'll like it if you only try it. Now come, child." The old woman smiled so sweetly that Susan began to doubt what she had feared. The soothing words floated around inside the girl's head. "Have some candy and think about it," Mrs. Happy said. "You don't have to use your number today. But why miss out on all the fun? All the other children are having fun, fun, fun. Don't you want to join them? Take my hand. It's so easy to join in."

Then the old woman touched Susan's hand. Susan jerked back. The old woman's hand was cold and reminded Susan of the one time she had been brave enough to touch a dead snake. That dead snake felt just like Mrs. Happy's touch. "I'm not taking that number or any of your toys," Susan said.

"Maybe not today then," Mrs. Happy said. "I can see that it's been a long day for all of us. But you'll be back. Young or old, clouds or sun, you'll come back, to have some fun."

"I won't take anything from you, today or tomorrow or ever!" Susan said. "And neither will they." Susan grabbed a doll from Katherine's hand. She threw it on the sidewalk at the old woman's feet. Katherine swallowed her Sweet Temptation candy. A sour look crossed the little girl's face.

"Don't you touch my toys!" Katherine yelled. "Never! Don't you touch them!"

Katherine bent over and picked up the doll. She stuck her tongue out at Susan, then pushed past her. "I'm going home," Katherine said.

"Me too," said Lois. "I don't want to be around Miss Susan Grouch."

"Me neither," John said. He looked at Susan. "You shouldn't be such a spoilsport, Susan. You really ought to act your age."

"John, wait," Susan said. But the other children ignored her. Susan looked at Mrs. Happy. The old woman tapped the black number card in her hand and smiled at Susan.

High overhead, Nail cawed and flew slowly down. Mrs. Happy held up her arm. The crow landed on it. "Sure you won't change your mind?" Mrs. Happy asked. "It'll be lonely, when you're the only one without my toys. You'll miss the fun."

"Miss the fun," echoed the crow.

"You haven't won yet," Susan said.

"I don't know what you mean, my child," Mrs. Happy said. "But your family likes those toys. They took them freely as they were given. They gave permission. And that's all I really ask of anyone. I just want their permission to help them and give them what they really want deep down inside themselves. And now I have that permission from your sisters and John. You can't change what's been done."

"We'll see about that," Susan said, even though she feared it was too late for her family. But she knew the Three Kings were powerful, so in spite of herself she said, "You just wait."

"I will wait for you, my child," the old woman said. "And that won't be long. See you at the fireworks tonight."

Mrs. Happy smiled once more and then walked back into her store. The crow fluttered on her arm. Susan felt like crying for a moment. If Mrs. Happy and Goliath Toys were able to get these toys into the hands of all the children in town, how could one girl on a bicycle stop them from enlisting them all at the fireworks that night? She picked up her Spirit Flyer and got on.

Mrs. Happy waved to her from inside the store. Susan turned her head quickly away. She began to pedal but realized she didn't know where she wanted to go. She wanted to catch up to her sisters and John and tell them about the dangers of the toys and what she had seen in the mirror, but she realized for the first time that they wouldn't understand unless they were riding their Spirit Flyers. They needed to see the deeper danger for themselves.

Susan pedaled slowly past the town square. Across the grass, over by the row of roses, the Cobra Club was checking their wounds and arguing about what had gone wrong. They went silent when they saw the girl and her old red bicycle. Susan looked carefully at them, but none of them made a move. They watched her as if she were a ghost or an alien from outer space. Susan shook her head, then rode slowly toward home.

HOW TO
STOP
A LEAK
· · · · · · · ·
19

Mrs. Happy wasn't the least bit happy. She stood in front of the toy store and paced back and forth. She had been stewing ever since Susan had left without having her face processed onto the number card and puppet. Barry was supposed to have met her a half-hour ago, but he was too busy smiling like a game-show host at the party at his house. The old woman was worried.

"Where is that boy?" she asked the crow.

"Late, late," Nail the crow croaked. "The boy is late."

"Very late indeed," Mrs. Happy said.

Then she saw Barry cut across the street on his Goliath Cobra Deluxe.

The Faster Blaster and the Combo-Gizmo were bolted onto the handle-bars next to the black box. She opened the door for him as he knocked down the kickstand.

"You're late," Mrs. Happy said with a frown. "I get upset with children who are late."

"Keep your wig on," Barry said, as he walked into the toy store. "I got here, didn't I?"

"Watch your mouth, young man, or I may give you toad lips," Mrs. Happy said. "How would you like to eat flies and beetles the rest of your life?"

"What?" Barry said. He was about to laugh, when he saw that the old woman was serious. "Look, I'm sorry that I'm late. There's a swell party going on at my house today and I just forgot. Before that, we got to blast John Kramar. We got him good out at the dump. I even got an extra bicycle out of the deal. But when we tried to blast Susan Kramar, you won't believe what happened with that ugly Spirit Flyer bicycle of hers."

Barry told her the whole story but Mrs. Happy didn't appear surprised at all. "The whole club is worried," Barry said. "They want to know how she could do something like that. And I told them that you promised us something better than a Spirit Flyer. You said you'd give me a bicycle that could make a Spirit Flyer look like a kite."

"You do have a problem," Mrs. Happy said, "in listening to what other people say. I said that there are bicycles that are much more powerful than Spirit Flyers, and that it would be like comparing a jet to a kite."

"Well, where are they?" Barry demanded. "I'm afraid those guys will all want Spirit Flyers and that will be the end of the Cobra Club."

Mrs. Happy stared at the boy. She stared for such a long time, that Barry grew uncomfortable. Then she stared at the crow. "You must remember," Mrs. Happy said, "that what those boys want is not a Spirit Flyer, but the things a Spirit Flyer will do. We mustn't underestimate the power of those old bicycles, my boy. But not just anyone can ride a Spirit Flyer. There are all sorts of silly conditions and regulations that the enemy has put on them. You can't ride them for long without running into problems. They are unreliable bicycles. No one would have any more fun if everyone had a Spirit Flyer. The government knows this, but you must prove that to your club. And once your club sees that, then they will want a Goliath Super Wings. With a Goliath Super Wings and Goliath Toys like the Combo-Gizmo and the Faster Blaster, you could do much more than a Spirit Flyer will ever do."

"Why can't we just get a Goliath Super Wings then?" Barry asked.

"Because it just isn't done that way," the old woman said. "Haven't you ever heard of the Point System?"

"No," Barry said. "What's that?"

"What *are* they teaching these children in school?" Mrs. Happy asked the crow. "The Point System. That's why you have your number cards. To keep track of your Goliath Credit Points. With enough Goliath Credit Points, you are allowed bigger and better toys and so forth. That's the Point System. Everybody uses it."

"I never heard of it," Barry said.

"Fiddle-faddle," Mrs. Happy said. She looked over to Nail the crow. "And the Bureau expects me to shape this town up."

"Really, I never heard of the Point System," Barry said. "How does it work?"

"Well, I suppose you could compare it to school work," Mrs. Happy said. "If you do a certain amount of work at school, you get one hundred points or an A. If you do less work, you get fewer points, like seventy-five or a C."

"I get it," Barry said. "It's sort of like making money."

"Exactly, my boy," Mrs. Happy said. "I should have known that cold, hard cash is the best example. In this case, however, you need Goliath Credit Points and money. And you need many more points than you have now. But there's a problem."

"What?" Barry said.

"Susan Kramar, of course," Mrs. Happy said. "She's causing a leak. She didn't take her number card or any of the toys. In order for the Goliath Point System to work best, everyone has to play by the rules. It's a sort of game. She's been a naughty girl and broken the rules. She's upset the system. And until she's stopped, the points can all dribble away, like water out of a leaky bucket."

"A leaky bucket?"

"Yes, and Susan Kramar is that leak," the old woman said. "She'll make it much more difficult unless she's stopped. A chain is only as strong as its weakest link. We could just ignore her, I suppose, but that can be dangerous. The whole order . . . I mean chain, could break. You and the rest of the town's children are only on Level One according to the Point System rules. And because you're only on Level One, none of you qualify for a Goliath Super Wings."

"But what about me?" Barry demanded. "I'm Number One. Don't I get better stuff?"

"Not until the girl is dealt with," the old woman said.

"But I still couldn't stop her," Barry complained. "None of us could with that crazy bike of hers."

"Even so, she must be dealt with," Mrs. Happy said.

"Why don't you stop her?" Barry said. "We already tried blasting her, but . . ."

"She got away, didn't she?" Mrs. Happy said for him. "I know all about it. Excuses and more excuses. As I told you before, we in the government are like generals, and you are the soldiers. There are many things we can't do. We need a human . . . I mean a soldier like yourself to help us."

"But we tried getting her," Barry whined.

"Well, I've been playing this game too long to be blamed for mistakes like yours," Mrs. Happy said. "You are Number One, after all. If you want to stay at Level One for the rest of your life, that's up to you. But you won't stay Number One. We can get another more cooperative child."

"Hey, I'll always be Number One in this town," Barry said. "Who's going to stop me?"

"The leak, that's who," Mrs. Happy said. "As long as she's breaking the rules, the Toy Campaign will be in danger. The Point System will be harder to put in place. Sooner or later, the loyalty of your club members will stop when they see you are a failure. Then someone else will be Number One."

"They will not!" Barry almost shouted.

"Then take care of this problem," Mrs. Happy said. "I can't do it for you. Then again, maybe I know someone who can."

"Who?" Barry asked.

"John Kramar, of course," the old woman said. She laughed. "I should have planned on him from the start. He's been a most cooperative child since I came to this town."

"You aren't promoting John Kramar over me, are you?" Barry asked. Worry was written all over Number One's face.

"You catch onto the Point System fast," Mrs. Happy said. "I knew you would see how it works. The Kramar boy isn't being promoted above you. Not yet, anyway. But he is close to the girl and can be used. It's standard government procedure. The closest ones can do the most damage. Family members are most effective. Since he may be falling down a hole soon anyway, why not take someone else along?"

"I'm not sure I understand," Barry said.

"That's because you are a silly, stupid boy who's stuck on Level One because you didn't do your job correctly today," Mrs. Happy said. "Just remember there are other boys the government is considering for Number One."

"Well, they'll have to fight me first," Barry said, making fists with his hands.

"That's better," Mrs. Happy said. "I was beginning to think I had made a mistake about you. You need to be going back to your party. Take some more candy and be sure to give it to all your friends. We can talk about the Point System later. Once you know how the game is played, you'll love it, I can assure you. After all, you are Number One."

"That's right," Barry said. "And I'll blast anyone who tries to take my place."

"Well, you can just relax for now," Mrs. Happy said. She patted him on the head. "Your job is done for the moment. When you're ready to go on to Level Two, you'll be the first to know. If we can get the problem of Susan Kramar settled today, then you may be moving up the ladder of success faster than you know. After the fireworks display in a few hours, many questions will be answered and our victory will be in hand. A few more surprises remain to complete a wonderful first day in the Toy Campaign."

Barry smiled his new smile. He wanted to ask more questions, but he knew it would only make the old woman mad. He took the candy and followed her out the front door.

SUSAN'S
FAILURE

· · · · · · · ·

20

Susan hadn't gone straight home after
she left the toy store. She had pedaled around town, trying to think how
she could convince John and her sisters of the dangers she had seen
in the old broken mirror on her bike. One of Susan's friends, Mary Jane,
had asked her to go to the party over at the Smedlowe's, but Susan had
refused. She hadn't told Mary Jane about Barry trying to bomb her with
firecrackers because she didn't want to explain about how she had
escaped.

When she finally got home, she went to her room and read in *The
Book of the Kings*. Even though she read a long time, she didn't find

any information to help her. The words of the old book seemed dry and hard to understand. Susan finally decided to just go talk to her sisters. She put the book and her glasses on a shelf.

Her sisters were playing with the new toys in their bedroom. They were giggling and laughing, but when Susan opened the door, they stopped. "Don't you know how to knock?" Katherine demanded.

"Yeah," Lois said. "You just can't come banging in here like you own the place."

"All I did was open your door," Susan said.

"Well, close it and get out," Lois said.

"But I want to talk to you about the toys," Susan said. "I think you should take them back. I don't think they're good toys."

"Of course they're good toys," Katherine said. "Whoever heard of a bad toy? The only bad toys I have are the ones that aren't any fun and are boring."

"Like you," Lois added.

"Why are you both being so mean to me?" Susan asked.

"You're just mad now because you didn't get any toys like my Sissy Sassy doll," Lois snapped. "So why don't you just shut up? Sissy Sassy says it."

And with that, Lois pulled a string on the doll. She pointed the doll's face at Susan and let go of the string. "Sissy Sassy says 'Shut up, stinky,' " the doll said in a mean little voice.

Susan's eyes went wide with surprise. Katherine, who was watching, laughed. Susan stared at the little doll. The doll's face had a little smirk on it and the open, unblinking eyes seemed to be mocking Susan.

"I don't think that doll is very nice," Susan said. "Maybe we should show it to Aunt Bernice."

"Get lost, Susan," Lois said and stuck her tongue out. "Sissy Sassy says it."

The little girl pulled the string once more on Sissy Sassy. She pointed the doll toward Susan and let go of the string. "Sissy Sassy says, 'Get lost, ugly,' " the doll said. Then the doll began laughing. Katherine and Lois began laughing right along with the doll. Susan felt the tears coming to her eyes and ran from the room.

She slammed the door. Her aunt Bernice was carrying a bag of groceries into the kitchen and saw the whole thing. She frowned at Susan.

"Susan, you know you shouldn't be slamming the door like that," Aunt Bernice said. "You apologize to your sisters. And then help me in the kitchen."

"But they have terrible mean little dolls," Susan complained. "They got them for free at the toy store. There's something wrong with those toys."

"Are you sure you aren't just mad because you didn't get any of the toys?" her aunt asked. "Lois and Katherine said that when it was your turn in line, you refused to go in. Now go and apologize to your sisters. Then you can help me."

Susan opened the door. The laughter stopped. "I'm sorry for slamming the door," Susan said quickly. "But I really think we should talk about your toys and about the fireworks. I'm not sure we should go tonight because . . ."

"Go away," Lois whispered, so Aunt Bernice wouldn't hear. "Sissy Sassy says go . . ." Susan shut the door when she saw Lois pulling back the string on the little doll.

"That's better," Aunt Bernice said with a smile. Susan was quiet as she helped put away the groceries her aunt had bought. She lined up the rows of canned goods carefully on the pantry shelf, trying to think of a way to tell her aunt about the strange new toys. Aunt Bernice talked about the parade and what a big mess it had turned out to be.

"I'll be making sandwiches to take with us to the fireworks show, her aunt said. "Don't be running off."

"Ok," Susan replied. "But I think you should look at those new toys I don't like them, and I think something's wrong with them They have these dolls called Sissy Sassy and they say mean things "

"You're just imagining things, Susan," her aunt said, getting the mustard and mayonnaise from the refrigerator. "I think everyone's imagination has been running wild the last few days. Those kinds of dolls say cute things. You're just taking it the wrong way."

Susan sighed. She saw it was useless to try and convince her aunt. She left the kitchen and went out to the garage.

The big garage door was open. John was pumping up the tires on his Spirit Flyer. He looked up at Susan, but didn't say anything. He went back to pumping. Susan had left her Spirit Flyer out by the front steps. She went to get it and pedaled into the garage. She sat on her bike and watched John work.

"What did you say were the names of the toys you got?" Susan asked.

"I got a Goliath Faster Blaster and a Goliath Combo-Gizmo," John said. "But I don't think it's any of your business."

"Why are you being so mean?" Susan asked.

"Why are you being so nosy?" John grunted.

"I saw something in the mirror after we left the dump, John," Susan said. "I saw some of it before I rescued you. Then I saw more of it later. I saw the black window thing. It's huge. It must be half the size of that whole pit. You knew it was there all along, didn't you?"

"So what if I did," John said. The boy stopped pumping. A slight hissing noise came from the front tire of his Spirit Flyer

"Why didn't you tell me?" Susan asked.

"Because I was . . . I was busy," John replied.

"What other things haven't you told me?" Susan asked. "I think that there's something wrong with the toys. I saw them in the mirror too. You saw what will happen at the fireworks tonight too when you disappeared that time. but you've said so little about it. Why?'

"You don't know where I went or what I saw for sure," John accused her. "I thought there might be something wrong with the toys, but I've changed my mind. I didn't want to make a mistake like you They're only toys after all."

"But there is something wrong with them, don't you see?" Susan asked. "While I was looking at the mirror, I saw where we had been outside the toy store. I saw the big line of kids. At first they looked normal, but then I saw how they were all connected. There was a chain between each of them, John. Like an invisible chain. A chain from the Deeper World. And the chain was pulling them along. And it'll be like that tonight too. You can't go. Those are the chains Grandpa was warning us about."

"Pulling them where?" John demanded.

"They were being pulled into the toy store just like a dog on a leash or a puppet on a string," Susan said. "It was as if they didn't even know it."

"That's because you're just seeing things," John said. "I was right there and I didn't see any chain. Really, Susan, I think you've been out in the sun too long. You're the puppet brain."

"How can you say that?" Susan asked. "I've told you how you can see deeper in those old mirrors. I also saw something else, though it was only for a second. That big chain we saw at the dump was more than just a chain."

"Sure," John said. "What was it?"

"It was a backbone," Susan said seriously. "The backbone of a huge black snake. I'm telling you, John, I could see the scales, its horrible red eyes and everything. And then it grew and grew. It was a snake bigger than the Centerville courthouse. It could eat that trash pile at the dump with one bite."

John looked carefully at Susan. He swallowed. His face appeared to go pale. "You're just seeing things," John blurted out.

"But if you would put the mirror back on your Spirit Flyer, you would see it too, John," Susan said. "Why don't you put it on? Then you would see the danger. You would see how that chain could be part of a snake. That snake is made of shadows and darkness not of this world. It's like it's invisible, yet right there. The chains are the same way. And so are those black windows. They're like holes or windows into the Deeper World I think. Don't you see? And that's why we've got to stop Katherine and Lois and Roger and the rest from going to the fireworks display tonight. I'm not exactly sure how it will work, but that old woman will get permission to sign people up to something Tragic. If you would attach the mirror on your Spirit Flyer, then maybe you could see how those black windows and the toy store and the fireworks and how everyone is linked together by those . . ."

"I'm busy and I don't have time for mirrors," John said. "But I am going to put something useful on my bike, this and this." John held up the Goliath Faster Blaster and the Goliath Combo-Gizmo. "Barry and the Dead Men's club blasted me with these and I plan to get even. They're at Barry's house now at his stupid party. I bought firecrackers from Roger. I'm going to show them that two can play at their game, only I'll win. With a Spirit Flyer, I can sneak up on them and speed away so fast they'll never know what hit them. Then I'm going back out to the dump and get what's mine."

"No, you can't," Susan said firmly. "A Spirit Flyer won't work that way," Susan said. "And I think you'll be in big trouble if you try it too."

"Of course, it will work," John said, though suddenly he didn't look so sure. "It's my bike. I'll make it work."

"Just like you made the gear lever work?" Susan asked.

John paused. He started to snap back at Susan then stopped. He looked down at the old bicycle and then at the Combo-Gizmo and the Faster Blaster.

"You'll be making a big mistake if you put those things on your Spirit Flyer," Susan warned.

"Who are you to tell me what to do?" John said. "I'll do what I want, when I want. Just stay out of my way."

John put the pump on the workbench. He wiped his hands on a rag. The tires of the old red bicycle were very low on air even though John had been pumping for fifteen minutes. He figured he'd be flying along once he got started anyway, so he wouldn't need much air in them.

Susan cringed when she saw him pick up the new black toys. He lifted the Goliath Faster Blaster and set it down on the handlebars of the Spirit Flyer. "John, don't," Susan cried. But John didn't listen. He used a wrench to tighten the bolt that held the Faster Blaster on. A great hissing noise began coming from the Spirit Flyer as steam rose from the handlebars where the Faster Blaster touched.

"You're hurting it!" Susan cried. She rolled forward on her bicycle to stop him. John had a wild look in his eyes. He held up the wrench in a threatening way when he saw her coming.

"What are you talking about?" John demanded.

"The hissing noise," Susan said. "Don't you hear it? Don't you see the steam?"

"You're really crazy," John said. He went on tightening the bolt. The noise sounded almost like a cry of pain.

"You don't hear or see that?" Susan asked. "You're hurting your Spirit Flyer."

"I don't know what you're talking about," the boy said with determination. "You've been hearing and seeing things for days. Just leave me alone. This is my bike and I'll do with it what I want."

"I may not know how those awful things work," Susan said. "But I do know something about Spirit Flyers and I know you can't mix things with them. I read about that in *The Book of the Kings.* Only Spirit Flyer instruments work on a Spirit Flyer."

For a moment, John didn't seem so sure of his plans of revenge on the Cobra Club. Then a frown spread across his face. "That's just an old book," John said. He twisted the wrench with a savage yank.

Susan couldn't stand it anymore. She reached over and grabbed his arm to make him stop. He pushed her hand away.

"You're changing, John," Susan said. "Something's going wrong. It must be because of those toys. I can almost see . . . I did see! Just for an instant. I saw those chains . . . they're on you right now. It's like I saw right into the Deeper World."

Susan rubbed her eyes. John looked down at his chest, then felt around his neck. A frown crossed his face. "You've gone off the deep end," John grunted. "I'm leaving." He hopped on the Spirit Flyer. He dropped the wrench on the floor in a clatter. "See you around," John sneered. He pushed Susan out of the way and headed down the driveway on flat squishy tires. Susan put her hand over her mouth as she watched him leave. First she failed with her sisters, and now she failed with John. The only thing she was sure of was that something awful was about to happen.

THE LIGHT
ON THE
BIKE
· · · · · · · ·

21

John Kramar rolled down the driveway with the two Goliath toys attached to the handlebars of his Spirit Flyer. Susan wasn't the only person watching John as he turned toward Barry's house. Other eyes were very interested in the changes coming over the boy.

Mrs. Happy was at the back of the toy store looking through the black window. Nail was perched on her shoulder. They had both watched John put the Goliath Faster Blaster and Combo-Gizmo on the old red bicycle. Mrs. Happy was working two dark hooks inside the window as if she were knitting. The old woman smiled as she heard John arguing.

"See how the flame burns in the boy," Mrs. Happy said. "The darts were well aimed, if I do say so myself. The fire has been building. We'll eat a feast of ashes tonight."

"Ashes from the flame," the crow croaked.

Mrs. Happy leaned forward and blew through the window. The deeper blue flames burned invisibly inside John. As Mrs. Happy blew, the flames burned brighter.

"It will either work or I'll get a bicycle that will make them work," John was saying.

Mrs. Happy laughed. "This may be easier than we first thought," the old woman said, watching John pedal down the street. "After the campaign is really rolling properly and the Point System established, the Bureau may set me up as district manager. Or maybe I could get an even better position back in television. My number should go up considerably higher, the ashes of success."

The old woman laughed, then she laughed some more. She worked the hooks faster.

"See you around," the boy sneered and rolled down the driveway on the flat tires.

"He's almost there," Mrs. Happy whispered. "Just a little more and . . . gotcha!"

As John rolled out of the driveway, he reached down to adjust the Faster Blaster. The moment he touched the odd new weapon, the Spirit Flyer skidded to a halt beneath him.

Susan, who was still watching, was just as surprised as John. She knew he hadn't touched the brake. He pushed on the pedals to make it go forward.

"Come on, you stupid bike," he muttered. And at that instant, the bike began moving. But instead of going ahead, the old bicycle began moving backward!

John yelped and held on. He pushed on the brake, but that only made the Spirit Flyer move faster. The wheels were already braked tight, but the bike was still moving backward, as if being dragged along. The tires skidded down the street, leaving long zigzagging black marks on the pavement. As the bicycle moved faster, the skidding tires began to smoke.

John shook the handlebars. But when he tried to move his hands, he couldn't. They seemed to be glued fast. John yelled, looking back at Susan. He shook the handlebars some more.

"John!" Susan called. She had been watching with her mouth open. She had never seen such an odd sight. John had already skidded backward a block before Susan could even think to move.

"Help!" John called, skidding around the corner. The smoking skid marks burned on the pavement. The bike moved even faster as it carried the boy out of sight.

The stinky black smoke of the melting tires covered the boy like a cloud. The tires skidded away, leaving big holes. Then the rubber inner tubes wore quickly through to the bare metal of the wheels. The wheels scraped and flashed like two sparklers. John shifted in the seat to look backward, to see where he was going. He jerked his hands once more, but they seemed to be welded solid to the handlebars.

"Not again," John whimpered to himself. "I didn't even touch the gear lever. I don't even have it on the bike." Then the boy looked down at the Goliath Faster Blaster and the Combo Gizmo stuck on the handlebars where the old mirror and rubber horn belonged. The bike moved faster. The noise of the grinding wheels made his head hurt. John kept looking for someone to help him, but the streets were empty. The whole town of Centerville seemed stopped, frozen in time or asleep. Within a few minutes John had hit Crofts Road and the bike headed out of town, still going backward.

"Come on, Susan," John said. "Or somebody." But the bike just sped up leaving a long trail of sparks shooting into the air. The wheels screeched as the bicycle turned the corner onto the old dump road, then bounced across the bridge over the Sleepy Eye.

When John hit the bumpy dirt road on the other side of the bridge, he felt as if he would fall off for sure. But that wasn't possible because his hands were still stuck to the handlebars. Dust rose up in a flurry as the wheels dug into the ruts and potholes. John bounced so much he felt as if he would just shake apart. The dump was coming up fast on the left.

The bike turned into the dump area, spraying dust and gravel everywhere. John hoped that his ride was finally over. But the old bike was being dragged straight toward the smoking mountain of trash. Fire had burned away half the pile. Smoke and ashes smoldered in the place where John had been digging earlier. A blackened set of wire bedsprings lay in a heap on top of the ashes.

The bicycle went backward right into the smoking trash. Finally, the bike slid to a halt on the dirt. A cloud of dust hung in the air.

That's when John saw the toys. Right in front of him, at the end of the path not more than fifteen feet away were boxes and boxes of toys. Shimmering in the ashes, they seemed miraculously untouched by the fire. The toys were so bright and new, they almost seemed to have a life of their own. John smiled greedily for an instant.

Then he noticed the black window. What was left of the back wheel had stopped at the edge of the strange black surface. The boy had been staring so hard at the toys that he forgot everything else for a moment. John suddenly felt cold.

The air was split by the screeching sound of freight-train wheels grinding on gravel. John knew without looking what he would see. The giant chain moved slowly up out of the trash through the boxes of toys. The heavy links slid toward the boy on the battered bicycle. That's when the eyes and the skin and the scales of the huge snake slowly appeared around the chain in an almost ghostlike way.

The snake slowly circled around the boy and bike. The blank red eyes didn't even seem to see John. The head burrowed back through the ashes and trash, and then disappeared down into the black window as

ıf it were slipping into an oily black pond.

The snake's body pulled tighter around the bike and boy, squeezing them out over the pool of darkness. John yelled and squirmed, kicking at the sides of the ghostly serpent's body. But the pull from the Deeper World was stronger. The battered bike and boy were sucked into the darkness in an instant . . .

Susan started down the driveway after John as soon as he was dragged around the corner. She had heard a horn blow, but she hadn't stopped to listen. As she hit the street, a bolt of black lightning swept in front of her face in a screaming cry. She fell sideways as the big bicycle went down.

Nail flew back up into the air and then dove down again as Susan tried to get up. Susan put her hands up to shield her face. She dropped the bike again. The crow flew higher and circled above her. Susan was about to go get a broom from the garage to protect herself, but decided against it.

"I've got to help John," she murmured to herself. She picked up the old red bicycle once more and hopped on. The horn blew again. The crow dived, but went wide this time. Susan started pedaling.

The street was filled with smoke from the burning skid marks which made the girl cough. She didn't question why there would be so much smoke, she just tried to go forward. But she could barely believe her eyes when the boiling skid marks on the road began to writhe and wiggle like hundreds of snakes. Susan stared at the bubbling tar of one of the skid marks in front of her. Right before her eyes, it wiggled off the pavement toward her bicycle. And there wasn't only one, but a whole streetful of smoking, writhing snakes. They came at her with red eyes. One squirmed its way into the spokes of her old bicycle before she could dodge it. She braked.

Susan reached down to pull the snake off, when the hissing open mouth struck at her hand. Susan jumped off the Spirit Flyer. Another skid-mark snake wriggled toward the old red bike, circling in and out and around and over the frame. Susan jumped back as the snake claimed the bicycle.

"If only someone were here," she said. But the street seemed strangely empty for that time of day. More and more of the black smoking snakes oozed toward the fallen bicycle. Susan felt sickened to see the snakes attacking the Spirit Flyer.

"Please help me," she said. Then holding her breath, Susan ran into the midst of the snakes and grabbed the handlebars. The Spirit Flyer seemed to right itself at her touch, throwing the snakes off. In a flash, Susan was on the old bike. But snakes were coming back, oozing and smoking, their staring red eyes fixed on the girl.

As if by instinct, Susan reached down and touched the old broken headlight of the Spirit Flyer. Right on top was a little lever, the on-and-off switch. As the skid-mark snakes slid toward her in smoky trails, Susan turned the lever.

Like a mighty rushing wind the light whooshed on, so bright the rest of the town seemed suddenly plunged into night. The snakes squealed and popped, sizzling back into smoke in an instant inside the beam of light. Susan squinted. When she was sure the snakes were gone, she flipped the lever. The town seemed to return to normal.

"Thank you," she said softly to the old bike. The only signs of the snakes were a few lines of sticky tar here and there on the pavement. Susan pedaled the Spirit Flyer a little way, then aimed for the clouds. She rose over the neighbor's roof and gained speed. But John was nowhere to be seen. She passed over the town, then sped on. She braked in midair and waited.

"I can't find him," she whispered to the old bike. "But I know he's in danger." The wheels began to turn by themselves. Susan held on as the bike gained speed. Soon they were flying out over Crofts Road. When they passed over the Sleepy Eye, Susan knew they were headed for the dump.

Susan held on as the Spirit Flyer zoomed over the forests and fields below. The bike flew closer to the ground as the dump came into sight. The girl and old bike landed on the ground just inside the gate and sped toward the smoking mountain of trash and ashes.

Susan stomped back on the brake, skidding up to the edge of the huge black window. She looked down. Staring back up at the girl from the darkness were two dark reflections of herself. One face was almost transparent and laughing. The other face seemed solid and calm.

"This is the end, Susan," the laughing face said. "You've reached the edge of your fears. You have to stop now. Sorrrrrrrrryyyyyyyyy!"

"You're lying," Susan said in spite of herself. "You're not real."

"You get what you see, little double me," the ghostly reflection replied. "You're afraid and I'm on your side. Forget it. John's not worth the trouble. He's chosen his chain. Run away. Before it's too late."

Susan looked around. For the first time she noticed some shadowy dark scales on the ground and saw the sliding track of the giant snake in the dust and ashes. The scales, if they were real, were bigger than plates.

"If only Grandfather Kramar were here," Susan said. "I don't know what to do."

"The choice is yours, Susan," the solid calm face said. "It's not by might or power, but by my Spirit. The kings are calling you. Listen and don't be afraid. Go forward in the light as he is in the Light. The light, Susan."

"Nonsense," the other face replied, and laughed. "You're smarter than that. You can't do it. The pull of the chain is too strong. If you enter the darkness, you'll be pulled away too. John's already a slave Run away now, before the chain tightens . . ."

Susan leaned over the edge. The voices bounced around inside her head in echoes that got louder and louder. "The light, Susan ' she said to herself from deep inside the darkness that surrounded her. "The light. The choice is yours."

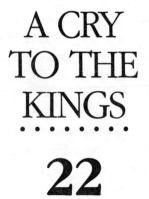

A CRY
TO THE
KINGS
. . . .
22

The moment John was sucked into the darkness of the black window, he felt the heavy pull of the chain dragging him deeper and deeper. "Not again," John moaned, remembering the first time he had disappeared after putting the gear lever on the Spirit Flyer in the wrong way. As if returning to a bad dream, he passed through the same darkness. From his past journeys, the boy knew he was traveling inside the Deeper World, yet looking out at the regular world. Even though he was moving backward, he sensed he was traveling into the future.

John looked over his shoulder and saw the town of Centerville approaching in the distance. Even though it was bright daylight when his backward ride began, he could see fireworks exploding in the darkness.

And just beyond the bursting skyrockets, on the edge of town, a gigantic snake reared high into the sky like a writhing tornado. Through the darkness, the boy saw the gleaming red eyes of the serpent. As John approached, the huge eyes turned toward him and the tiny bicycle. The snake opened its mighty jaws.

John stepped back on the brake, but the Spirit Flyer was dragged faster. That's when John noticed the chain on himself. It was wrapped around his neck and stretched out behind him, into the sky, straight into the mouth of the serpent. The snake was pulling him in, link by link.

The bicycle was dragged backward, deeper and deeper. John yanked his hands free from the handlebars and grabbed the chain so he could throw it off. But the pull of the chain was stronger than he ever imagined. As soon as he grabbed it, he was yanked right off the old bicycle.

And as soon as he left the seat, the Spirit Flyer began to fade away. John felt a cold panic in his stomach as he saw the old red bicycle get dimmer and dimmer until it looked like a ghost of a bicycle.

"I have to make it stop," he said, flexing all the might in his eleven-year-old arms. But the force of the chain only grew stronger and stronger. The mouth of the snake grew larger as he was pulled toward it. And the closer he got, the more the Spirit Flyer just seemed to fade away until nothing was left of the old red bicycle.

Since he didn't see the Spirit Flyer, the chain seemed the only thing left to hold on to. By then, he was directly over the town. The fireworks were popping all around him as the chain carried him straight into the mouth of the waiting serpent.

"Noooo!" he cried. He was so afraid, his heart felt as if it were coated in ice.

As he traveled deeper inside the darkness, John saw a faint blue light before him. And as he got nearer to the light, he began to hear a steady pounding noise. The pounding grew louder as the light got brighter. Smoke moved below his feet as if he were standing on clouds.

Then the pulling stopped. The chain was heavy around his neck. The dark links hung down his chest, the ends disappearing into the smoke. John felt hope for an instant. Then the chain jerked tight, pulling him forward. He tried to dig his heels in to stop the pull of the chain, but his feet slid through the smoke. The chain tugged him again, jerking the boy forward, off balance.

No matter how he fought it, nothing could stop the pull toward the blue light. As he was pulled closer, the smoke cleared away enough for him to see.

Someone, whose back was turned, was in front of him. The chain pulled the boy closer. The figure was standing in front of a huge mountain of glittering, gleaming objects.

"The toys," John said. He stared at them as if he were staring at all the treasures of the world gathered in one place. Then the figure in front of the toys turned around. With a smile, he pulled the chain and John stumbled closer.

"Welcome," the ghostlike figure said. John gasped. The person holding the other end of the chain wore John's face.

John rubbed his eyes. For a moment, the boy felt as if he were looking into the reflection of a nightmare. At first he thought the figure was a Daimone, but the other boy seemed too real, too much like John. With growing despair, John realized he was back in the exact same time and place as the last time he disappeared. Except instead of repeating history, he seemed to be repeating the future.

"I knew you would be back," the ghostly John said. "You'll always come back. We made a deal. You don't break the Order of the Chains. No one breaks the Chains. You'll always come back to me, because deep down, I am you."

"No," John said. "This is me." John tried to look away from the odd image of himself, but couldn't.

The figure, still holding onto the chain, walked over to the pile of toys and more toys. He picked up a baseball mitt at the edge of the pile. Then he tossed it toward John. "Catch!" the ghostly John yelled and then smiled as John's hand automatically reached up to catch the mitt. The mitt was an expensive brand, made of the finest leather. John admired it so much that for an instant he forgot where he was. He put it on his left hand. The chain rattled.

"That's what you came back for, isn't it?" the ghostly John asked, then laughed. "Now you can have it. You can have all the toys you want from Toy Mountain. Everyone in town will be here soon, so you better choose now. They've been down at the new toy store getting a taste for the toys. Everything is free just for the asking, once you pay a tiny admittance fee. Just think, toys galore. All you want forever and ever."

"I can have anything?" John asked. He thought he almost remembered the answer before the other John could speak.

"You can have anything," his ghostly image said with a smile. "How about one of these?"

The ghostly image stooped down and picked up a toy locomotive from the edge of the pile. He tossed it to John who caught it with the baseball mitt. The train was a beauty.

"You can get the rest of the train in a little while," the ghostly John said. "Now we have visitors."

John looked behind him. Through the smoky darkness, he saw them coming one by one. The children of Centerville were in a long, long line that disappeared into the darkness. Barry and the other members of the Cobra Club were the first in line. Each boy wore a large loose chain that was locked around his neck. And all of these chains were connected from child to child. The children's eyes were closed as if they were walking in their sleep. Even so, smiles spread across their faces as they got close to the pile of toys, as if they could smell them.

"The blind leading the blind," the ghostly John said cheerily as he looked on the children. Then he smiled at John. "And you're the blindest of all. You tried to break the Order of the Chains. But the chains aren't broken. They are being forged together. You'll never escape their power. You belong to me, here. There is only one kingdom in all the worlds, and it belongs to Treason."

"I belong to the Kingdom of the Three Kings," John said weakly.

"Silence!" his image shouted. The boy shuddered, rattling the chain. "Look at the chain and where you are. You pulled yourself from your world into ours. This is where you really live, deep down, isn't it? Right here at the foot of Toy Mountain. I told you that you would return. You never really left, not since you put on the gear lever. And you will bow to me here forever. No one escapes. After all, you made the deal."

"What if I change my mind?" John asked. Then he looked at all the toys just waiting in a heap. The boy's heart trembled at the thought of actually owning such a mountain of treasure.

"You're still going nowhere," the ghostly John said with quiet satis-faction seeing the boy's greed. He laughed. "In fact, you give out the toys to the others. I'm tired. You are me and I command you to do it. Give away the toys, one by one."

Behind him, the sleepwalking children came closer and closer. They murmured as their hands lifted up to receive the toys. "I won't," John said. "I won't do any of this. I'm going home."

The reflection yanked the chain hard. John flew forward, tripping over toys. He fell at the feet of his image. The ghost sneered at him. He yanked the chain once more. "You are home, boy," the ghost said with a wicked smile. "Don't you get it? See how comfortable and familiar the chain feels."

"I don't like this," John said. He struggled to his feet. The train and baseball mitt had fallen out of his hands.

"We can always make an even better deal, you and I," the reflection said soothingly. "You can always cooperate with the chain, and it won't seem so hard. In fact, you'll soon think of it as a golden necklace. There's great power in the chain, if you would only see it. Once you use a little, you'll want to use a lot. And the power grows." The image of John laughed. "You must remember one thing. The chain is long. Long and impossible to see, unless we will it so. I can pull you back here anytime, even if I let you go. I warned you the first time with the gear lever and all the other times, but you didn't listen. So if you don't cooperate this time . . ."

"What?" John demanded. "What will happen?"

"You'll be back here in an instant," the ghost said. "I've told you before that you would be back, didn't I?"

"Yes," John admitted to himself.

"I am you. Nothing has changed," the other John said. He gave the chain a tug and John trembled under the dark pull. "You were never free from the chain. I will always be here, at the other end. When I pull, you will obey me. You only thought you were free."

"But I am free," John blurted out. "The King Prince broke the locks. I know he did. The lock is gone."

"Then why are you here?" the other John asked, shaking his head. "You must not have been good enough for the kings. They only want the best. They could never want a weakling like you, could they? Where is your silly little toy bicycle now? See? You gave up on them so they gave up on you. I guess you just weren't good enough for them in the first place. But they're impossible to please anyway." The ghost roared in laughter. He pulled the chain so tight that John again fell at his feet. "Now it's your turn," the double whispered.

Then out of nowhere it seemed, an old woman walked down the pile of toys. She was smiling as she came to greet the children. In her left hand was a tablet of papers. In her right hand was a long shiny needle. It was Mrs. Happy, just as John had remembered her from the first time. He looked at the needle in her hand and tried to run away, but the ghostly John yanked the chain tight. He struggled like a fish hooked on a line as the old woman came closer.

"I've come to collect," she said with a smile. "Time to make it all official, in writing, in blood." John struggled wildly against the dark chain. But the image of himself held him tight. "All it takes is a drop," the woman said to John. "Just a drop a day, keeps the fear away."

She reached the bottom of the pile of toys. She walked over to John quickly. "Be a cooperative child now," Mrs. Happy said. "You wouldn't be here if you didn't want the toys. And I'm practically giving them away for free. Just a single drop of blood for your signature. A mere permission form. Where else can you get a deal like that? And this time you can take the toys back with you."

John looked down at the new toys, just waiting to be used and played with. For the first time he was beginning to see the doubts he had in his heart about the Three Kings. At once he felt like a traitor for even thinking such thoughts.

"You are a traitor," the ghost John quickly agreed with the boy's doubts. "That's why you still belong to Treason. Now let's get on with it. All you have to do is donate one drop now. When you do it a drop at a time like this, it doesn't seem so bad. This is home, my boy, so you might as well have all the fun you can. It doesn't get any better than this."

"No!" John said. He swung the chain at the ghostly image of himself. But he spun in a circle so the chain wrapped around his body. His arms were pinned to his side. He felt totally helpless and frustrated. Bitter tears began to fall. The old woman moved closer. She picked up his hand and felt the hot warm fingers, full of blood.

"Look at the little boy cry," the ghost mimicked in a baby voice. "Does he want his mama and dada?"

"Yes," John cried bitterly. He called out to the kings in his heart.

"Daddy, daddy," the reflection sneered. "What a baby you are. No wonder the kings didn't want you. I hate you myself. Think about that, you sniveling traitor."

"I don't want the toys. I won't sign," John cried out. In his heart of hearts, he cried out to the kings once more. Mrs. Happy waited, licking her lips, the needle an inch away from his right index finger. But in a deeper quiet place, the tears of the boy's heart were heard.

INSIDE
A BEAM
OF LIGHT
· · · · · · · ·
23

Susan trembled at the edge of the huge black window, staring down into the darkness, unsure of what to do. Two faces that looked just like herself claimed to be the girl's true reflection. She knew she would have to choose one voice to follow.

"Save yourself!" the dark reflection snarled.

"The light, the light," her other self said. "Go in the light."

"Oooh, why can't I decide?" Susan whispered. "Help me."

Then the angry transparent face disappeared into the darkness. In an instant, Susan knew what to do. She let go of the brake. "Not by might or power, but by my Spirit," she repeated to herself.

The Spirit Flyer plunged forward into the darkness. A horn blew as she was sucked under, and that's when Susan flipped the switch on the old light. In a blast of music, the light cut through the darkness. Susan opened her eyes to the Deeper World, and what she saw made her heart race with fear. The beam stretched out before her. And at the end of the light, a gigantic black snake wriggled and writhed as if in pain. The beam of light cut into the dark side of the serpent, stabbing it like a spear.

The old red bicycle hummed forward inside this beam of light. As she got closer, Susan saw John far away, inside the snake. The old red bicycle sped closer. In an instant she was at the foot of Toy Mountain by her cousin.

Susan stared at the ghostly reflection of John and the real John. For a moment she was puzzled. She also saw the line of sleep-walking children. The children seemed almost transparent and ghostlike as they froze before the tunnel of bright light. Susan sensed that she and John were in the future, somehow, in the Deeper World. At the same time, Susan felt a sense of urgency, as if this future was about to happen.

Mrs. Happy was standing near John. The old woman had stopped moving the instant the light hit her. Susan wasn't surprised to see her in this place. Mrs. Happy seemed transparent, and Susan could see right inside of her. A dark ugly spot covered the old woman's heart like a shadow. The only sign of life was in the two fiery red eyes that watched Susan. Off in the darkness, more red eyes had gathered to watch as well.

"John?" Susan asked.

"Oh, Susan," John said "The chains pulled me here. Only he said I pulled myself. He said I can't leave, that I have to stay here with him. I made a deal."

The ghostly John squinted and held his hands up to block the light, as if he had been blinded. He fell onto the smoky floor and crawled toward the darkness.

"I still hold the chain," he called out. "I still hold the chain." Then he was gone. There was growling and groaning in the darkness beyond. The red watching eyes of the others moved no closer, the light seemed to scare them away.

Susan held out her hand. John reached and touched it. "Let's go," Susan said. "It's ok now. They can't keep you here. Even if you did make some kind of deal, they are liars. And you don't have to honor a contract made of lies."

"But I lost the Spirit Flyer," John said, shame filling his voice. "I knew I shouldn't have made that deal not to use the instruments. Now I've lost the bike too."

"Well, it hasn't lost you," Susan said. She pointed. John looked down. He hadn't noticed, but he was sitting on the old red bicycle. John looked amazed, then smiled.

"Let's go," Susan said. "This place, whatever it is, gives me the creeps."

"I've been here before," John said quietly. The chain was still around his neck, and the ends led off into the darkness where his reflection had hidden. But for the first time, the weight of the chain was gone. "My bike is a mess," John said, looking at its melted tires.

"You better hold my hand," Susan said, reaching out toward John. The boy nodded and got a firm grip.

"Let's ride," John said.

Susan turned the bicycles around. She only began to pedal when there was a humming sound. The bikes shot forward, washed in the joy of the light

THE TARGET
HOUR
ARRIVES
• • • • • • • •

24

The children and all the townspeople gathered out by the baseball field at the Centerville school on the east side of town.

The crowd formed just outside of right field. The band set up on chairs just beyond the foul line in right field itself. Far beyond the band, way out on the other side of left field, the volunteer fire department stood ready by the waiting fireworks.

The people came in cars and pickups and bicycles and on foot. They gathered under a darkening sky. The clouds hung low and threatening, no one knew what they contained. Yet the people came, putting down blankets and big ice chests for their evening picnics. Some families backed their pickup trucks toward the field and let down their tailgates for makeshift picnic tables.

This year was different than all the ones before, however, in that many children brought their new Goliath toys to the field. Everywhere you looked there were girls clutching dolls and holding balls and boys with Faster Blasters and action figures and all sorts of things. Yet none of the children were playing together. Most of them seemed tense and suspicious, as if someone were about to snatch their prized possessions away. The faces of the children looked as uncertain as the clouds overhead.

Katherine and Lois and Aunt Bernice arrived with the crowd. The children had come in the car and argued all the way about whose Sissy Sassy doll was better. Aunt Bernice, who was upset because John and Susan had apparently run off somewhere against her explicit instructions, scolded the two girls and tried to ignore the problem. She had made ham and cheese sandwiches and was quite hungry since it was past supper time.

"I wonder where John and Susan are?" Lois asked.

"Who cares?" Katherine replied. "I don't like Susan anymore because she said all those mean things about my dolly."

"Yeah, she is snooty," Lois agreed. Aunt Bernice spread out an old quilt on the grassy ground. Katherine and Lois both wanted to sit on the left front corner and argued about it until Aunt Bernice told them no one could sit on that corner. Both children stood in an angry silence, blaming each other for the punishment.

Lois pulled the string on her Sissy Sassy doll and pointed it at Katherine. "Sissy Sassy says you made a big mistake, ugly!" the little doll chirped.

"I did not," Katherine said. "And don't call me ugly."

Katherine pulled the string on her doll and faced it toward Lois. "Sissy Sassy says you stink and need your diaper changed," the little doll said. The blank, staring doll eyes almost seemed to squint for a moment.

"I do not!" Lois screamed. She was ready to scratch Katherine as hard as she could when Aunt Bernice came between them. Just then the band began to get ready. The conductor stood on a small wooden platform and waved his baton. The national anthem began and all the people stood up proudly. High above, a black crow flew in circles, looking down on the crowd below. The cloudy sky rumbled with distant thunder.

The band played song after song and the crowd applauded each patriotic tune. The sun went down and the sky got dark quicker than usual because of the clouds.

Then the mayor stood up to speak. A microphone on a pole was brought over. "Thank you, band. Thank you, Mr. Brooks, our fine conductor," the mayor said. The crowd clapped. A clarinet squeaked.

"As the band plays their last number, the fireworks will begin," the mayor said. The crowd clapped and cheered. "But this year we have a special treat. By now, we're all aware of the newly remodeled toy store in town. The new name in entertainment and fun is Happy Toys." The children in the crowd screamed and clapped their approval. "We're especially proud to welcome Mrs. Happy, the new owner of the store. She is associated with Goliath Toys, the fine company which is sponsoring a special display of fireworks this year. I've been told we are in for a treat." More applause and cheers drifted through the crowd.

"And speaking of Goliath Toys," the mayor said proudly. "Many of you may know that Goliath Industries, the parent company of Goliath Toys, has recently bought the old factory here in town. In the near future they will be gearing up for production to complete several government contracts." A huge roar of applause spread through the crowd as the mayor beamed. He took out a handkerchief and wiped his face.

"Centerville, of course, welcomes Goliath to our community with open arms," the mayor said. "Besides this delightful display of fireworks, Goliath has also planned some other beneficial gifts to our community which will also be announced in the near future. But let me now introduce our newest, and already one of our most beloved citizens, especially by you children—Mrs. Happy." The children all stood on their feet as Mrs. Happy walked over to the microphone and into the spotlight. The adults also stood up and clapped.

Mrs. Happy looked out over the crowd and smiled warmly. At that moment, big tubs of Sweet Temptations candy were being passed through the crowds. The children took handfuls and stuffed them in their pockets and their mouths. "Thank you for your kind welcome," Mrs. Happy said, her voice echoing out of the speakers. "It's fitting that on this day that celebrates freedom, we are gathered together. Every Independence Day is special, but I know this will be a day long remembered for me. Your welcome and permission to share the celebration with a display of Goliath fireworks means more to me than I can express. So without further delay, on with the show!"

The children clapped in thunderous applause. The crowd cheered. Many children held their toys over their heads and waved them. Mrs. Happy smiled as she looked out over the faces. She carefully searched the crowd, looking for Susan and John Kramar. Just then, Barry Smedlowe and the Cobra Club rode their bicycles between the cars and trucks and quilts, all the way to the front of the crowd.

Mrs. Happy stepped away from the microphone. The big field lights went dark at that moment. Except for a few small lights focused on the band, the field was dark. As the band played a rousing Sousa march, the fireworks began. A rocket shot high into the air and exploded into an umbrella of stars that were red, white and blue. A breeze scattered the stars across the sky. The citizens of Centerville cheered with satisfaction. They ate and drank, toasting their freedom and all the good things they possessed. Another rocket exploded against the darkness into many lights. Mrs. Happy looked on the sea of upturned faces and smiled with so much pleasure that for a moment her eyes seemed to glow red.

At the same time, Susan and John were in the garage at home working on his Spirit Flyer. When they shot out of the Deeper World, the beam of light led right to the Kramar's garage. "We need to fix your bike," Susan said. "That must be why we were brought here."

"But don't we need to go warn the town about how Mrs. Happy will enlist everyone tonight, just like we saw her doing in the Deeper World?" John asked.

"Yes," said Susan, "but we can't make the same mistake of trying to do the kings' work with an incomplete Spirit Flyer."

John nodded. The Spirit Flyer was a mess. John felt terrible when he realized how badly he treated the old bicycle. The children went to work quickly. John took off the Goliath Faster Blaster and Combo-Gizmo. Then they replaced the melted tires of the old red bicycle with the good tires from Mr. Kramar's Spirit Flyer.

"Dad won't care," Susan said after they were done. "You can get him some new tires tomorrow. We've got to get out to the school."

"You put on the gear lever," John said and looked down at his sneakers. "I made such a mess of it last time."

"It's ok now," Susan said and smiled. She patted John on the back. "You can bolt on the light and horn and mirror. I'll hook up the generator too."

"I wonder what it does," John said.

"Who knows?" Susan said. "But we'll find out when we're ready, I suppose. Let's hurry."

The children worked quietly, passing wrenches and pliers back and forth. Susan strung the gear lever cable to the back wheel, looking at her own Spirit Flyer as a model. As she tightened the last bolt on the generator, a distant boom filled the air. The children ran to the front of the garage. "The fireworks have begun," John said. "We need to get over there soon."

"We've got to keep working," Susan said seriously.

"I just need to attach the horn," John replied. Another boom echoed in the distance. As Susan worked, she whispered her urgent and deepest wishes to the kings.

Out at the field, the last regular rocket shot up and exploded into a

star which exploded into more stars. The crowd clapped. In the darkness, the mayor grabbed the microphone. "And now for our very special display, courtesy of Goliath Toys," he said. His voice was drowned out by the cheers and applause of the crowd. A stirring breeze blew across the field.

The fire chief lit the fuse for the Goliath display. The first rocket went up higher and higher and higher until everyone thought it was probably a dud. Then with a big boom, the rocket exploded just below the clouds into what seemed like a thousand purple stars. Then those stars popped into more stars. The crowd clapped at the wonder. The whole town of Centerville seemed to be covered with burning stars. Then someone shouted, "Look, it's words!"

And so it was. In fiery letters, the stars spelled—THE TOY CAMPAIGN. The crowd murmured with wonder. It only lasted for a few seconds, then the stars faded to ashes.

The ashes trickled down over the whole town as another rocket went up. This time, the stars formed into the shape of a tiny person. "It's a doll!" they shouted. Then the doll faded to ashes which dropped down, still smoking.

The next rocket went even higher and made the image of a bicycle. And at that moment, the wind blew and the bicycle began to move across the sky until it faded into smoke and ashes. Though most smoke moves upward, this smoke drifted down over the crowd. A few people coughed, their eyes watering.

Another rocket whizzed upward. This time it exploded into the image of a puppet. The breeze made the puppet seem like it was dancing on its strings before it was lost in the wind. The crowd applauded wildly, though more and more were coughing from the smoke.

Then a rapid burst of explosions sent several rockets into the air. Every expectant eye was on the darkness when it exploded into glorious pictures of toys of all sorts. There were bicycles and dolls and balls and bats and trains and airplanes. No one had ever seen such a display of fireworks. Children pointed and licked their lips as they sucked on the Sweet Temptation candies. For a moment, everyone seemed to forget they were only looking at dots of light. With their eyes blurry from the thick smoke, something about the images made them seem to be more than toys.

And while the images of toys floated high in the air in sparkling fire, another series of rockets went shooting up into the sky for the final display. A gust of wind whipped through the sky when the rockets exploded higher than all the rest in a horrible flash and deafening roar as loud as bombs in battle.

The crowd waited anxiously to see what image the burning stars would make. Everyone gasped when they saw the giant hood and the long curvy body of the cobra. "Wow!" Barry said to Doug Barns.

The giant snake swayed over the edge of town, with the breeze almost making it look alive. It spun and turned as the wind suddenly picked up. The crowd clapped and applauded and shouted at the wonder above them. But the burning stars still didn't go dark. The wind only made them burn brighter as the snake of fire began twisting wildly in the black cloud-filled sky. With an open mouth it moved toward the lingering display of all the toys.

Then to everyone's amazement, the snake seemed to eat the display of toys with a tragic bite.

"Wow!" Barry Smedlowe said, his eyes reflecting the red and purple stars above him. By then, smoke was thick in the crowd. Ashes fell down over the people as if the towering snake were shedding its scales. Then in a whoosh, a ball of fire seemed to shoot right up through the belly of the snake and out its mouth, shooting like lightning through the sky. A boom as loud as thunder cracked the air. Someone screamed. Then the twisting snake rose taller into the air.

"I don't like this," the fire chief said to his assistant. "Get the hose. That thing looks like it's coming down."

The people in the crowd were all looking up when the giant snake came twisting down like a tornado of fire. The eyes of the serpent glowed, and the mouth seemed to open once more as it fell toward the earth. The wind was suddenly fierce on the field.

All at once, everyone began to scream. The siren of the fire engine began to blow which seemed to increase the panic. Some people began to run, but most could only stare up into the sky, hypnotized by the red eyes.

The snake of fire whipped back and forth over the crowd, as if waiting to strike. Then with the sound of rockets, the giant mouth came down, the jaws opening wider and wider. The mouth alone seemed bigger than the whole Centerville school building.

The firemen ran toward the crowd as the snake fell. So much smoke was in the air that most people couldn't see clearly by that time. The band members rushed toward the crowd. The jaws of fire opened behind them as the head of the shadowy serpent hissed downward through the smoke and panic.

Then the bottom jaw of the snake touched the earth, singeing the grass with fire. And at that instant, the town of Centerville froze in time. In that split between normal ticking seconds, the darkness of the Deeper World had broken through like an ugly dream.

Everywhere, all over the field, people stood like statues, stopped as if asleep. Some were balanced on one leg as they were running away. Others had their mouths open as they looked upward with their eyes closed. The whole town was like one big photograph—no sound, no movement. Only the snake burning on the field seemed alive, its huge fire-red eyes looking on the helpless people before it.

But not all was stillness. Mrs. Happy came walking out of the crowd of sleeping statues with the black crow perched on her shoulder. "The target day has arrived," she said to the bird with satisfaction in her voice She held a long hook in her hands about the size of a garden hoe. Her hook was connected to a chain which was connected to a puppet about two feet tall that wore the face of Barry Smedlowe. The chain went on from the Barry puppet to the next puppet, which looked like Jimmy Roundhouse which went to the next puppet, Number Three, who was Doug Barns. From puppet to puppet, the chain traveled on, connecting them in the order of their numbers. Each puppet wore the face of the child who had given permission earlier that day in the toy store. One after another, the puppets marched, each bearing the face of a child of Centerville, each linked together by the chain.

"Ah, freedom," Mrs. Happy said as she pulled the marching puppets across the field to the open mouth of the waiting fiery serpent. "This is more like it. When they think they are most free, they are the most blind to their slavery. What a moment! Add a few toys and we'll get decisions for darkness. Blood on the dotted line."

The Barry Smedlowe puppet marched on deep into the mouth of the snake. Mrs. Happy released her hook and the puppets kept marching, one after another, deep into the belly of the dark serpent.

As the puppets marched, she walked back to the little wooden bandstand that the conductor had stood on. She waved her long hook in the air, like a conductor listening to silent music. One by one the puppets marched into the deep darkness of the gigantic snake as Mrs. Happy conducted, a smile on her face.

The last two puppets to be dragged along bore the faces of little Katherine and Lois Kramar, number five hundred and sixty-two and five hundred and sixty-three. The chain in front of the Katherine puppet was held together by a broken link. Yet with continuous pressure, the chain pulled the puppet along as if it weren't broken at all. Behind the last puppet, which wore the face of Lois Kramar, a length of loose broken chain dragged on the dirt. A pile of fluff and doll hair and cloth was all that remained in the last puppet.

Mrs. Happy stopped when she saw the mangled chain and the destroyed remains of the last puppet. "The boy, the boy," she gasped. "Where's the boy? His puppet is not intact. The girl I knew, but not the boy."

"The Order of the Chains unravels," the crow taunted. "Target day? Hah! Perhaps you collected signatures before they were given."

"Shut up, you featherhead!" the old woman snapped. Her eyes glowed red as she searched the crowd of Centerville citizens trapped in time. The parade of puppets moved past her. Mrs. Happy jumped off the bandstand. She looked around quickly once more.

"We must hurry, they can't have broken through," she said to the crow. She turned back to the snake. As the puppet of Lois Kramar marched mechanically into the darkness, a blue light began to glow deep inside the burning serpent.

Through the smoke-filled air and darkness, glistening new toys appeared deep inside the snake. A jumble of baseball gloves and balls and bats and action figures and dolls and all sorts of delights, fresh out of their boxes, were heaped together like a mountain of treasure. The Barry Smedlowe puppet reached the mountain first since he was the Number One puppet.

And the instant the little puppet hands touched the first toy, a spark shot through the links of its chain as if it was plugged into an electric socket. The spark shot down the chain from puppet to puppet. The little two-foot puppets began to run all at once, each one pulling harder on the one behind.

Mrs. Happy smiled, then looked out in the crowd. The real Barry Smedlowe had begun to move. He walked forward, his eyes shut as if asleep. He was followed by Jimmy Roundhouse, who also appeared asleep, followed by the rest of the Cobra Club. And after the Cobra Club came the other children, one by one, in the order of their numbers.

The children sleepers formed a long line as they marched toward the gaping mouth of the fiery serpent.

"Hurry!" Mrs. Happy commanded. She stared out through the smoke-filled darkness. The adults of the town all stood still, helplessly locked in their sleep. Yet not all were quiet. A few adults made sounds of weeping and crying. "Quickly now," the old woman commanded. One by one, the children walked away from their families and joined the parade of sleepwalkers as their numbers came up. On they marched, both arms reaching out, yet holding nothing. A dark, almost invisible chain linked the children together. The deeper they walked into the hungry serpent, the clearer the chain appeared.

TWO
SPIRIT
FLYERS
· · · · · · · ·
25

Susan Kramar tightened the bolt beneath the old cracked mirror and dropped the wrench. "There," she said. "Let's go."

"I hope we're not too late," John said.

As Susan pushed her Spirit Flyer down the driveway, she jumped on. John was right behind her. "I'm glad to be working with you instead of against you," the boy whispered to his old red bicycle.

Before Susan's bicycle reached the end of the driveway, the big front tire rose swiftly into the air on its own. John's Spirit Flyer lifted off right behind her. "Hang on!" Susan called as her bicycle climbed higher and higher. John nodded.

The bikes shot over the roof of their neighbor's house as they turned toward the school. High above the houses and street lights below, the old red bicycles picked up speed as they flew toward the east side of town.

The school wasn't far away. John's Spirit Flyer pulled up along Susan's old bike. The wind felt crisp and refreshing on their faces. But as they got closer to the school, they flew into the cloud of smoke that hung over the field and surrounding area. The smoke stunk as if a thousand graves had been left open to rot.

"It seems so quiet," Susan said. "And what an awful smell!" They shot past the last row of houses. The baseball field came into sight through the hazy smoke.

"Look!" John said excitedly. He pointed. Even through the smoke, both children could see the resting serpent of fire and darkness.

"My goodness," whispered Susan as they sped closer. "It's just like it was in the Deeper World . . ." Just then, the huge fire-red eyes of the serpent looked up at the two small flying bicycles. The mouth that was almost closed, opened wide.

"Hang on tight," Susan yelled as the bicycles dove into the fog.

Mrs. Happy looked up when she saw the snake's mouth opened. "Curses," she yelled at the crow. She ran toward the snake, waving her long hook. "Take them, you fool, take them!" The snake began to rise up, its jaws lifting off the ground just before Mrs. Happy arrived. About twenty of the sleepwalking children remained outside of the snake's mouth. They dangled in the air, chained together, like beads on a necklace. Yet they didn't awaken. They seemed as weightless as vapors, their eyes shut, their faces blank.

At that moment, Susan and John zoomed right under the huge snake's jaw.

"No, no!" Mrs. Happy screamed from the ground. "He can't have broken the contract. The chain was repaired!"

The children soared into the air, as the snake turned, struggling to find them. The old red bicycles circled around the head which had flattened like a cobra ready to strike. The sign of the circled X burned in white fire on the snake's chest as it reared up. The chain of sleep-walkers swayed out of the mouth like a piece of noodle.

"What do we do?" John called to Susan.

"I don't know," Susan shouted back. She stared at the huge scales of the snake's head made of both fire and darkness. "Just hang on. Let the bikes lead."

The giant snake twisted, looking for the two magic bicycles. The Spirit Flyers flew as one, side by side, completing the circle around the huge head. They zoomed toward the gaping jaws. The eyes gleamed as a ball of fire shot out of the serpent's mouth toward the two riders.

"Look out!" Susan screamed. But before she could yank her handle-bars, her old red bicycle had already jumped to the side. A roaring flash shot past her like a comet. Susan quickly looked to her right and saw that John was safe too, the ball of fire had passed between them.

Susan gripped the handlebars tighter as she saw what was about to happen. The two old bicycles were flying inside the serpent's mouth. Far ahead in the distance, she saw the mountain of treasures bathed in a blue light. The sleepwalking children covered the mountain as they picked up the toys of their dreams.

John glided next to Susan on his bicycle. He looked at the toys longingly for a moment. "It's the same treasure," John said. "This is the place and time."

"But it isn't all the same," Susan replied, staring with wonder. "You're free now. You're awake. You aren't asleep or under any spell or contract. And you aren't chained to that ghost person. You have a choice, no matter what they told you. Remember, they're liars."

"But what do we do?" John asked. At that moment, the two red Spirit Flyers stopped midair in the belly of the dark serpent. The sleeping children were right in front of them, scrambling over the mountain of toys, filling their arms.

"The kings know what to do," Susan said, though she wasn't sure why she said it. The words had just come to her.

Then, as if out of nowhere, the children heard a voice terrible in majesty, deep and strong as thunder, the voice of a thousand oceans and waters. "Let your lights shine, for light drives out the darkness!"

Both children reached out toward the old broken headlights on their Spirit Flyers. Though their hands trembled, they pushed the switches at the same time. The light exploded from the bicycles in a crashing crescendo of music, flooding the deep darkness. In a blink of the eye, the snake and darkness had vanished before the blinding light.

When Susan's eyes could adjust, she saw that she and John were on their Spirit Flyers, on the ground, in the middle of the baseball field. The whole field was lit up brighter than noonday. In front of them was a mountain of smoking ashes. All around, the sleeping children stood like statues. Barry Smedlowe and many other children were in the pile of ashes. They reached down frantically, scooping up the ashes as if trying to hold on to a crumbling dream. Some children moaned in their sleep. And in the distance behind her, Susan heard the quiet sobs of weeping.

"My, my . . ." Susan whispered to John as she looked on the scene before her. Her cousin could only nod.

As Susan turned toward the sound of the weeping voices, she realized the great light on the field was caused by something behind her. Both she and John looked at the same time. But as she turned to the source of the light, she fell to the ground, fainting at the sight before her.

Susan lost track of time perhaps because there was no time at that moment. But when she awoke, the light was easier to see. John was lying on the ground beside her as if he too had fallen in a faint. Susan looked ahead and smiled. Then she reached over to John. "Wake up, wake up," Susan cried in a whisper. "He's here."

John opened his eyes and sat up. Like Susan, he could only stare at the person in front of them. No one had to tell them that they were looking into the eyes of the King!

CAUSE
FOR
CELEBRATION
· · · · · · · ·
26

Susan rubbed her eyes and looked again. Never in her life had she seen anything close to such a person. The great light wasn't just coming from him. It was him! He seemed to shimmer, yet one had the feeling that his light was covered greatly, as if he were holding back so they wouldn't be blinded by such light.

Both children, though still sitting down, bowed at the same time. There was no other choice. The stillness of the moment seemed to last forever.

"Don't be afraid," the King's Prince said. His voice, like his appearance, seemed restrained, as if he were speaking only in a whisper when he was capable of much more. "Stand before me."

The children struggled to their feet. Susan swallowed hard, staring.

She wondered if it was polite to stare, but nothing in the whole universe could have drawn her eyes away from his face. The Kingson smiled on them. Such a smile made her feel as if he had known her forever, and then she realized deep down that he really had known her forever. Susan didn't know whether to laugh or cry. She felt as if she would explode with the excitement inside.

"Speak," the Kingson commanded.

"I've . . . I've . . . read about you," Susan stammered. She immediately felt foolish and looked down.

John stepped forward to speak. But when he opened his mouth, his voice cracked and no words came out. He stared down, embarrassed.

"Fear not," the Kingson said simply. "The hour is coming when the Kingdom will drive out all darkness forever. But until then, there is work to do." His voice seemed so ordinary, yet at the same time, he seemed to speak with an authority and power that Susan had never known. His words cut straight through to Susan's heart in an electric chill of excitement. She felt a thousand things all at once, yet more than anything, she felt flooded with peace.

Though he stood in their midst, Susan had the sense that he was far away too. He seemed to stand in his own special sense of time, and was sharing that time with the two children alone. She couldn't see his feet, only light.

"Why did you come to us?" Susan asked in simple curiosity.

"I've never been gone, even from the beginning," the King's Prince smiled. "And where two or more children of our Kingdom are gathered, I am with them in a special way. Those who have eyes to see and ears to hear, know me."

"I guess I've just been reading *about* you," Susan said. "All I've known is the words and stories, but not you."

"Don't be dismayed, Susan," the Prince said softly. "You have done well. But you must know the life in the words, and I am the words of Life. To the ones who receive my gifts, I give more. To the one who

longs to see, I give the gift of vision. Cover your eyes with blessing. Learn to truly see me in the words, and also in that vision that surpasses knowledge."

Susan looked down. In her hand was a pair of old leather-and-glass goggles like the kind aviators used to wear. Embedded between the two eyepieces were three tiny golden crowns. On the straps was a simple label written in flowing white letters: "Spirit Flyer Vision."

"Thank you," Susan murmured in surprise. She had seen a pair of similar goggles before which belonged to Grandfather Kramar. She never dreamed she would have a pair of her own. She squeezed the old goggles tightly. The King's Prince smiled on her. Then he looked at John.

John quickly looked down. In a moment he felt filled with shame and began weeping, echoing the sounds of the weeping in the distant darkness. The boy saw in an instant the many times he had betrayed himself and others in the last weeks.

"Your tears speak well for your heart," the Prince said softly. "The time of weeping will end in joy. But be warned: the King gives good gifts so they will be received and used. Many are the battles that lie ahead. Without me, you can do nothing in this world. You have not learned that lesson. Instead, you have felt the pull of the chain and fallen into the darkness. You cannot serve the Kings and search for the treasures of this world too. I give you gifts more precious than gold. Take them, use them, and follow me."

The boy nodded, wiping his eyes. At that moment, John knew everything was ok. A great weight lifted off the boy.

"The pull of the chain is gone for now," the Prince said and smiled. "You wish to ask something?"

A look of surprise crossed the boy's face. He hadn't even formed the words of his question. "Will I always be making big mistakes like this?" John asked.

"Until all things are ready, there is danger in the pull of the chains," the Prince said. "But for every danger, you can escape if you look to me and the power I give through my gifts. The light of the Kingdom is stronger than darkness. But you must either choose my gifts, or you accept the pull of the chains."

"What about that other person that looked like John?" Susan asked. "And I saw one of me too. Are we two people deep inside? Will we always be fighting ourselves and the chains?"

Susan closed her mouth quickly. She wondered if it was proper to ask so many questions at once. But the Prince smiled and she knew he appreciated her interest. He wanted her to ask questions.

"You are only one, as I am one, and I in you," the Kingson answered. "But listen well. The locks on the chains are broken. The slave you were is gone, dead. You have a new life of freedom because of me. You are citizens in the Kingdom of the Kings."

"Then who is that person that looks like me?" John asked. "He seems so real!"

"That is the slave you once were, before the power of the chains was broken," the Prince replied. "Though the slave is dead, he can haunt you like a ghost. He is called the ghostslave and exists only as a lie. But a lie can become a danger when it is believed. The ghostslave feeds off your fear. He whispers lies that the chains still control you, that you are still a slave. If you believe these lies, then the ghostslave becomes stronger. He'll try to make all kinds of deals and contracts with you. But they're all lies. The biggest danger of the chain is that it can pull the ghostslave up out of the darkness so you are tempted to believe his tragic lies more than my truth. But fear not, I have overcome the darkness, and I am in you. Because of me, you have overcome the chains, if you will only discover it. You are free children of the Kingdom. Those who have eyes to see, will see."

The Prince was silent. The sound of weeping could be heard in the distance. "Who's crying?" Susan asked. Over in the crowd, many adults were totally asleep, but sobbing quietly.

"They cry for their children," the Prince said quietly. "And they cry for themselves, because they have tasted freedom, yet remained as slaves, asleep in the hour of need."

"You mean they were like me?" John asked. "Other people in town have Spirit Flyers, too, that they don't use?"

"Many in this town have wasted their gifts," the Kingson said. "In search of the toys and trinkets and other things, they miss the true treasures that are freely given. So many trade true treasures for a handful of ashes. And so they weep and are blind. They sleep, lost in the ashes of death. But these gifts don't have to be lost forever. You must use them, stir them up. Receive them fully with the love in which they were given. That is my message to you."

Then the Kingson turned. He stretched out his arms toward the townspeople. In the voice of a thousand blaring trumpets, he called out. "Awake, Sleepers! Arise from the dead, and light will shine on you!" The voice rocked through Susan so she could hardly stand. In a flash of light and music, the sky rolled back and thunder crashed. The two children fell to the ground as a mighty rushing wind passed over them.

Then light was gone as quickly as it had come. Susan opened her eyes. Everything had changed. People were talking and some were screaming. Smoke and ashes and sparks fell softly over the town like rain. All the people of Centerville were suddenly awake as the crack between time closed and the dream into the Deeper World had ended. Time began once more as if someone had started a clock. Everything returned to the same instant right before it had stopped. Only two things had changed. Susan and John and the two old red bicycles were out in the field, and Mrs. Happy and the crow were nowhere in the crowd.

The mayor of the town struggled through the commotion to the microphone. The panic seemed to be quieting. "It's all right," the mayor said. He looked up over his shoulder at the sky where the fiery serpent had been. "The fireworks are over, I think."

Someone began to clap, then another and another. Soon the applause was deafening. The big field lights were turned on. With the lights on, the people cheered because they didn't know what else to do. The mayor held up his hands and smiled.

"Well, that's a display of firepower we haven't ever seen in this town before," the mayor said, his voice creaking. "That was all planned, folks, to give us a thrill, so don't fret. The fire department had everything under control. I don't know how they do it, but it certainly had me on my toes. What a way to end our Independence Day. Goodnight, everybody."

The crowd cheered once more. Then people began moving around, packing up, loading stuff in their cars. The awful smelling smoke drifted through the crowd while ashes floated down. People still coughed. Everyone seemed in a better mood. Though many people had a nagging sense deep inside that something unusual had happened, the feeling was soon forgotten as they loaded up their cars and trucks.

Without speaking, Susan and John hugged each other. Then they picked up their Spirit Flyers and hopped on. They sat on the comfortable old seats and watched the people leaving.

"You think any of them knows what happened?" John asked. "It's like we saved them almost, and none of them even knows."

"No, and you probably couldn't tell them because they were asleep," Susan said. "I'm not even sure I understand very well, but I know things are ok, at least for now. We stopped whatever Mrs. Happy had planned, whatever was going on inside that snake. Because we were there to turn on the light, we helped break the Order of the Chains, at least for a time. That was what we were supposed to do."

"And I almost messed up the whole thing trying to get those stupid toys," John said sadly.

"But it's ok now," Susan said. She patted her cousin on the back. "I guess there'll always be toys just out of reach making us blind to the real treasures, like he said."

"Deep down I knew I should put the instruments back on the Spirit

Flyer," John said. "Grandpa told me to wait. And he warned me about those chains. I really did know better. But since I didn't wait and put the gear lever on wrong the first time, I got mad when it didn't work like I wanted. That's when I made the deal not to use any of the instruments. I figured they didn't really work, and besides, I thought I was going to get all those toys if I did what they told me. I believed their lies. Sometimes I think I'll never learn." John looked down. He gripped the handlebars of his Spirit Flyer. He sighed loudly.

"I read in *The Book of the Kings* that the best way to find out how Spirit Flyers work is to just use them," Susan said. "You learn by doing. I knew that, but I still didn't really do it. I wanted to wait and read how everything worked first. If they hadn't kept blowing the horn, I would have probably never woken up. Reading about the instruments was important, but you have to use them to really discover how they work."

"Well, the instruments are all on it now," John said with a sigh.

"Spirit Flyers are sort of like Christmas gifts," Susan said. "No one would leave their presents in boxes under the tree. You have to unwrap them."

"And play with them," John said and giggled. For the first time in a long time, he felt the joy he had once known of just sitting on the old red bicycle.

Susan held up the old leather goggles. She ran her finger over the three golden crowns. "I think we're going to like this gift," she said, beginning to feel the excitement of a child opening a present.

"Me too," John said. "Let's go home and try it out right now. Who knows what we'll see with them?"

"Race you," Susan said and giggled. In an instant the children were standing up on the pedals of the old red bicycles, speeding across the field. The faster they pedaled the Spirit Flyers, the more refreshed and happy they felt. By the time they got home, neither one cared who won the race. They had seen the Prince of Kings and that was cause enough for anyone to celebrate.

CLOSED
FOR
INVENTORY
· · · · · · · ·

27

The smoke and ashes that had rained down on the town of Centerville lingered through the night and the next day. Daylight came on July fifth with a fog of sour smoke hanging in the air

In the toy store, Mrs. Happy was staring into the black window on her desk, but all she could see was flashing lights and things out of focus. Two long black hooks lay idle in her hand. "Curses, I still can't see!" she screamed. The old woman rubbed her eyes. "Those wicked meddling children. How I'd like to get my hooks on them!"

"They did it again, did it again," Nail said. He hopped down on the desk and pecked at the old woman's hand. She swiped at him with a hook, but he fluttered away before getting hit. He perched up on a toy shelf and fluttered his black feathers. "You're in trouble now."

"Never," Mrs. Happy said. "The Bureau knows about these problems. The toys were distributed. So what if we are closed awhile? We'll have another chance to use the toys. They may have spoiled one target day, but we'll get our signatures sooner or later. Four little children can't stop us. We'll wear them down, little by little. The factory will be opening soon, school will start up. The Point System must go into place, with or without those brats."

"Dangerous," Nail warned. "That could be dangerous."

"We'll figure a way," Mrs. Happy said. "They'll bow to the Order of the Chains, you'll see. We just need to find the right link and the right hook. No one can resist the chains for long."

She stared back down at the black window, but the flashing lights and static continued. "We'll bide our time," Mrs. Happy said with a bitter smile. Just then there was a knock at the front door. The old woman walked slowly through the store. When she saw who was outside, she smiled.

Barry Smedlowe got off his bike. Mrs. Happy walked forward and unlocked it. Barry flashed his new and improved smile as the door opened. "Welcome, my young prince," the old woman said.

"Really stinks outside today, doesn't it?" Barry asked. "Those were great fireworks last night. It sure was nice of you to give them to the town."

"Yes, it was," Mrs. Happy said. "And I have so much more I want to give. Unfortunately, due to circumstances beyond our control, we are closed for inventory today."

"Closed?" Barry asked. "But you just opened."

"Well, that's the toy business," Mrs. Happy said. "Yet we will not be closed for too many days, I don't imagine. Our first concern is to give happiness to every boy and girl in this town, and we shall do just that.

But not today."

"Well, I know what would make me happy," Barry said with a greedy smile. "To get a look at one of those Goliath Super Wings bicycles. Can we do that today?"

"Well, we've had a few setbacks," the old woman said. "That's why we've closed to take inventory, so to speak. The government's plans for John and Susan Kramar didn't quite work out the way we had hoped."

"You can't rely on John Kramar for anything," Barry snarled. "I knew he'd mess up. I was going to tell you that yesterday. Just let him try to get points ahead of me. No one is more Number One than I am."

"Your position is secure," the old woman said and smiled. "At least for the moment. But we do need to be making arrangements for the future. We have a long hot summer ahead of us still. We are never closed to our most special customers, such as you. Maybe I'll have some new toys to show you in a few weeks, maybe not. Things are rather uncertain at the moment."

The president of the Cobra Club smiled. He scooped a handful of Sweet Temptations out of a purple bowl that was sitting on a shelf. He stuffed four of them into his mouth. Nail flew down and perched on the boy's shoulder. Barry offered a candy to the crow. Nail took it in his bill, then flew over to perch on the cash register.

"I better be going then," Barry said. He looked around at all the toys in the store. They were so bright and shiny and new that just looking made his heart beat faster.

"Come back tomorrow," Mrs. Happy said. "Maybe we'll be open for business then, maybe not. The interference we've run into could last awhile."

Barry grabbed some more candy, then walked past all the toys to the front door. Mrs. Happy locked it behind him as he went outside.

The air still smelled sour. Little paper-thin black ashes dotted the sidewalk and street like flower petals. Barry picked up one of the pieces of ash and saw that it was shaped just like the scale of a snake. All the pieces of ash had the same shape. Barry held the burnt scale up to his nose. "Yuck!" he said, throwing it down. "No wonder it smells like something died around here."

Then the president of the Cobra Club hopped on his bike and began pedaling down the street. As he rode, he practiced his new improved smile. The ashes blew like leaves as the thin wheels of his bike whizzed along.

THE GREATEST GIFT OF ALL

· · · · · · · · ·

28

Susan Kramar felt wonderful that Saturday morning. She had slept soundly all night long and woke up feeling rested and secure. Even Aunt Bernice's critical comments about the way Susan cooked scrambled eggs couldn't spoil the girl's mood. She walked around the house in a quiet, thoughtful glow that still lingered from the night before. Deep inside, Susan knew she would never forget her special meeting with the Prince of Kings.

After breakfast, Susan, John, Lois and Katherine met out in the garage. Susan had asked them to come and bring their Goliath Toys. Lois and Katherine were a little suspicious, but brought the two Goliath Sissy

Sassy dolls and two Goliath Chalkysqueaks.

For the first time in a long time, John seemed to be more relaxed and like himself. Ever since last night he had been more humble than usual too, which Susan appreciated.

"As I told you all last night, we have a little job to do this morning," Susan said. She was wearing her new glasses and for once she wasn't worrying about the way they made her look. "John, you go first."

John nodded. He got the Goliath Faster Blaster and Combo-Gizmo from off the workbench and put them out on the driveway. Then he got on his Spirit Flyer. The girls got on their Spirit Flyers too.

John rolled over to the two black toys, and pointed the headlight of the old red bicycle at them. "Here goes," he said. Then he flipped on the switch. The light burst out in a flash so bright, the children closed their eyes. But the flash only lasted an instant.

"Wow!" Katherine said. "They're gone."

A small pile of ashes was on the cement where the toys had been. John got off to look at the ashes more closely. In the middle of each pile was a tiny black cube about the size of a kernal of corn. He held one up for the others to see. "It's like a tiny piece of darkness, isn't it?" John asked. The other children nodded solemnly.

"I told you there was something wrong about those toys, deep down," Susan said simply. "They aren't right for people who have Spirit Flyers. Now it's your turn, Lois."

"Do I have to?" Lois whined. "Even though they stopped working last night, maybe they can be fixed."

"That's what I'm afraid of," Susan said. "Those toys are nothing but trouble and you know it, deep down. I don't think you can really play with them and with your Spirit Flyer too. Now is the time to decide what kind of fun you are going to have."

"That's not much of a choice," Lois said. She threw the two toys down before her. She flipped the switch on the light of her old red bicycle. After the flash all that was left were two smoking piles of ashes with little dark cubes in the center.

Everyone then looked at Katherine. She looked at her two Goliath toys and sighed. "Is this really necessary?" Katherine asked in her tiny voice.

"Yes," Susan said. "I read about it in *The Book of the Kings* last night with my new goggles."

"Did you really see him?" Katherine asked.

"Yes," John said softly. "And you will too one of these days. In fact, he's here right now, even though you can't see him. He's always been here. We just forget. You better do like Susan says. Those toys are trouble."

"Ok," Katherine said, though her voice was full of regret. "Since they don't work anyway, I might as well blast them like you guys. I just hope we're doing the right thing."

She tossed the two toys down on the driveway. She rolled around in a circle to get in a better position. Then she fiddled a long time with the headlight.

"Quit stalling," Susan said.

"Ok," Katherine said. She pointed the light from her small Spirit Flyer at the toys and flipped the switch. Like the others, it was over in an instant.

"That's better," Susan said.

"You know, I do feel kind of nice," Katherine said with a fresh excitement in her voice. "I had this crummy feeling, and now it's gone."

"The chains," Susan and John said together. "The Spirit Flyer broke their power." Susan and John looked at each other and laughed. "See, we are learning to discover things of the Deeper World," Susan said. "When I was reading last night, the book said that a person can learn a lot."

"I want to read some today with those goggles," John said. "I've got a lot to catch up on to know as much as you."

"Well, it's not a contest," Susan said softly. "I see now that I was trying to make it that way. Deep down, I sort of felt left out when you first got your Spirit Flyer and got the stolen bicycles back and everything. I guess I wanted to prove I was smarter or better than you or something. But the Spirit Flyers weren't given for that reason, but to help us as we go deeper on our journeys in the Kingdom of the Three Kings. I read that last night in the book. I had read it before, but it took me until this moment to discover what it meant. I'm sorry if I made you feel bad."

"That's ok," John said. "I have been acting like a real rat these last few weeks. Especially lying like I did. I hope you can forgive me."

The two children looked at each other, then smiled. Getting those things said was important. They both felt better.

"What about all the other Goliath toys in town?" Lois asked as she stared at the ashes in the driveway.

"Yeah," Katherine chimed in. "Should we go blast them with our Spirit Flyer Headlights?"

"Well, from what I read, they don't work that way exactly," Susan said and frowned. "Every person tries to get their own treasure, good or bad. If someone gave you their permission, then maybe the lights would work, maybe not. I think they would have to have their own Spirit Flyer and use it themselves. I couldn't use my light on your toys. You had to choose the light over darkness yourself. We don't understand all the ways of the Deeper World yet. But sometimes you can share the Magic of the kings with our Spirit Flyers, like we did last night when the light drove away the darkness of the big snake. We stopped that snake from swallowing the sleepers. But it's not the end of it. That was just one battle and the kings won."

"There'll always be more toys," John said, shaking his head.

"Well, what's wrong with toys?" Katherine asked.

"Yeah, I like toys," Lois added.

"Toys aren't the problem so much as which ones we want and how badly we want them," Susan said.

"I know I felt like a slave," John said. "I never really owned the toys under the trash pile, but they seemed to own me. All I could think about was getting them. But what was even worse is that I forgot the real treasures I already owned in my Spirit Flyer. You really can become blind to the gifts all around you. I know I did."

"Yuck!" Katherine said. "I don't want to be like that."

The children smiled at each other. Susan was about to suggest they all take a bike ride when Lois screamed. "Look, mommy and daddy are home!"

They jumped off their bicycles and ran to the street. They had practically surrounded the car before it stopped. Mrs. Kramar opened her door and carefully stood up. The children held back, uncertain. "Don't I get a hug?" she asked with a smile. In a second, she was surrounded by arms and more arms.

"Are you ok?" Susan asked.

"Yes," Mrs. Kramar said. "I'm doing much better now. And we should be having a new member in our family sometime around Christmas."

"Hooraaaaayyyyy!" Katherine yelled. "We'll have someone else to play with. Now I can be a big sister. I'll be a big help, Mommy."

"I'm sure you will," Mrs. Kramar said.

Mr. Kramar got a suitcase out of the trunk of the car. As he closed the lid, he looked at the six tiny piles of ashes on the driveway. "Have you kids been burning something?" he asked, and pointed at the ashes.

The children looked at each other, then began to laugh. "Not exactly," Susan said. "But some exciting things happened while you were gone. Just wait till you hear!"

"Yeah, I've got some things to tell you, too," John said. He looked down at his sneakers. Though he knew it wouldn't be easy to admit that he had lied, he felt relieved to have the chance to make things right.

"Well, let's all go in the house," Mrs. Kramar said. "I could sure use a cool glass of iced tea. Then you can tell us what you've been doing the last few days."

The Kramar family linked their arms together as they walked toward the house. Susan began explaining the adventure of toys and treasures, of chains and light. And the more she told, the more Susan herself understood the things she was telling. But this time she knew she had more than words, for she had discovered the greatest treasure of all, the Prince of Kings himself.